THE F-MAN HIMSELF

NICK NARIGON

HAYSEED PRESS LLC

HAYSEED PRESS

For Mosley and Dabney. We made it.

ROB ROBERT ROBBIE

July 7, 1994

Tell me, tell me, because I want to know. Everybody should know.

Look at me. Look at me now. Can you see? Everyone should see me.

Look at me run. Look at me jump. Look at me catch. Look at me run, leap, and catch.

I catch the ball. Cheer. Cheer. Everyone cheers.

When I drop the ball, no one cheers. It is silent.

"You should catch the ball," they say.

So I am quiet.

Nobody sees me.

So I get loud. I bang my drum. Listen to me. Watch me. Look at me.

Look at me hit the drum. I am loud. I get louder.

Bang. Bang. I bang the drum.

Watch what I can do.

When I am loud I cannot hear the silence.

I am the drummer. I am the corporal of the cartoon.

The drummer propels the spheres spinning. Follow me through the nonsense.

Here I sit. Down in the basement. My parents' basement. The room is a concrete bomb shelter. The far wall is lined with my dad's workbench. Assorted tools hang from pegs on the pegboard. On the opposite wall are metal shelves stacked with cardboard storage boxes. There are tents and sleeping bags for when we need to escape to the woods from this suburban bliss.

My high school friends are here for band practice. We'll be juniors this year. We practice our noise. If we are loud enough, the girls will hear our song.

In the concrete box, I am the man on the throne. My right foot rests on the Gibraltar ribbed bass pedal. My left foot maneuvers the hi-hat pedal. The slight tension keeps my ankles in their sockets. Wood-tipped Vic Firth drumsticks, 5A, are my weapons of choice. I twirl them like knives through my fingers. I am ready whenever they are. Fucking guitarists are so damn slow.

The drummer is the one everyone must follow. The drummer leads the soldiers to a steady tempo. With a sure warrior driving the beat, you rise over the hands in the field. Show them exactly what rock 'n roll is all about.

The drumstick in my hand is like a fine, felt-tip pen nestling between my knuckles. A machine of the simplest beauty. Intertwining threads of life and beauty to weave an intricate crochet of sunshine and fire. I create the magic. My wands if you will.

Me, my name is Robert Longley. Sometimes Rob. Sometimes Robbie. Don't call me Bobby.

I play rock 'n roll. Real rock 'n roll. Zeppelin, Doors, Skynard, GNR, that kinda shit. The stuff the white man stole from Robert Johnson and Muddy Waters. Only we were rich enough to buy amplifiers and mixing boards. One, rat, and three, tat. Pearl Jam.

At the age of 16, life is velvet and roses.

My friends Cody and Kiljoy, blonde mops bowed in earnest, stare at each other's guitars. Twang, Cody plucks the high E on the shiny red Fender his parents bought for his birthday. Kiljoy follows suit, watching Cody's nimble fingers. Cody reaches over and tweaks the tuning knob on the neck of Kiljoy's beat-up Squire, the one he bought at a garage sale for pocket change.

Little John's rock-solid bulk is perched atop his Peavey bass amp, fingering his four strings. His head cocked, tuning, his long floppy hair hanging over his bushy sideburns. Keith, the singer, has a silver screened microphone pressed against his lips. The feedback squeals and he mumbles over the lyrics written on the notepad in his hands. Mike, clad in a starch Gap polo, is sitting next to Keith, flipping through a *Playboy.*

"We about ready?" I ask to no one in particular. "I'm ready to fuckin' rock."

"Yeah, I think so," Cody says.

At that moment, recognizance. Cold anticipation. Confusion. Then we start playing.

Boom. I start with the bass drum. Tat I go with the snare. Boom-boom-pat. Little John joins in with the bass, moving up an F-minor scale. The trap set and the bass weld together. Steady, solid, strong, swelling. Everything else is frivolous. The frill on the curtains. The racing stripes on a Mustang. I lead, the Warlock.

Kiljoy follows John. He is still out of tune. Then Cody chimes in with the icing—a noodling guitar frill. Keith is last. The front man, but without the rest of us, he is nothing but a rooster on the roof. Granted, it's the singers that make the band. Where would the Stones be without Mick Jagger, the Doors without the Lizard King?

Keith is a clear tenor, but his lyrics could use some flavor. Of course, what does a fifteen-year-old know besides football and the fact that there are a couple of silky pubes tickling his dick? Hell, I just recently realized that most of the girls in my class are wearing grown-woman bras and blue eyeshadow.

Me, I know rock 'n roll. And I will be the King. The F-Man Himself.

Look at me now.

2

A BREATH OF HUMAN KINDNESS

September 9, 1996

Robert Longley glided down the sunbathed sidewalk of downtown Crawford Falls. Budding weeds flourished from the cracks. The hazy sun had reemerged from its short slumber behind the thick clouds on an early September Monday. A light crowd ascended on the town square. The paunchy businessmen in JCPenney suits were moseying about after an extra-long lunch break. The wined-up housewives were bustling from shop to shop in their knitted sweatshirts and jeans, dragging along toddlers in their Tommy ghetto gear.

It was a stark contrast from the crisp black suits and custom leather Robert had seen the pedestrians wearing out on Fifth Avenue.

Robert himself was wearing the Midwest uniform of a plain white T-shirt and a pair of worn khaki shorts that hung easily from his slight frame. A scruffy, red beard hid his boyish features. The sun enhanced the bloodshot twinkle in his eye and his ruddy cheeks shone with contentment.

Robert was intent on buying some rope. Just last month he returned from an ill-fated journey to New York City. Now he was seeking to escape from the deep funk in which he had sunk. Newly 19, Robert decided to quit the assorted recreational drugs he was consuming on the daily and shape his life into order.

After a weekend of camping, he came to the decision that rock-climbing would sufficiently raise him from his case of the mopes.

Robert had rock-climbed in his early teens when he was still with the Boy Scouts. But then it was a short 30-foot cliff with two advisors safely advising from the top and the nylon straps of his harness squeezing at his cowboys. Robert was now going to take his new endeavor to new heights on his own. Solo.

To do this, he needed some rope.

West Coast trends had reached Iowa a year late. The sleazy dive bars of downtown Crawford Falls were replaced by coffee shops. He had only been gone a month but already a sporting goods store took over the former Army surplus consignment shop.

Robert stopped outside the clean windows of the sporting goods store and peered inside. Soccer shoes were on sale. There had never been a soccer team when Robert was growing up in Crawford Falls. Now there was.

He entered the store through the automated doors and passed a clearance table filled with athletic shorts and T-shirts. Robert strolled through the store, inspecting each aisle as he passed. He finally found the camping section and browsed the hard-soled hiking boots.

The rappelling rope, crampons, and harnesses hung from hooks in the back corner. A light-haired girl tagging the carabiners smiled and stepped out of Robert's way. Her face was plain and sweet. Her curves were draped by her oversized polo shirt and work apron.

"Why do they have you hiding back here?" Robert asked her with a smirk.

"Excuse me?" asked the girl. She was startled by Robert's soft, polite voice.

"It's just that…," Robert demurred, his cheekbones flushing. "You have a pretty smile. I'm glad I found you back here."

"Oh, I don't know about that," said the shop girl with a nervous giggle. She huddled in close to the carabiners, her hands fumbling with the clips.

"I'm sorry, I embarrassed you," said Robert. His face brightened, revealing the gap between his two front teeth. "I think I embarrassed myself."

The girl laughed and flashed a bright smile at Robert.

"I was wondering if you could help me," said Robert.

"Of course," said the girl turning away from the merchandise and wiping her sweaty hands on her apron. "What are you looking for?"

Robert glanced at her name tag. He grinned even broader.

"Kristy," he said, reading the tag. "You know, you and my mom are the only two people I know named Kristy with a 'Y'."

"I got a friend back home that spells it the same way," said Kristy, blushing, picking at her name tag.

"Where is home?" asked Robert.

"Fort Dodge."

"You go to school here?"

"Yeah, I'm a sophomore at Western U."

"Oh really, what's your major?"

"Oh, well, bio-med engineering, I guess," said Kristy with another giggle. Her cheeks flushed again.

"You guess? That's some pretty tough shit just to be guessin' about," said Robert with a laugh. "You shouldn't be embarrassed."

Robert rested his pointed elbow on the shelf, leaning in closer to Kristy.

"I'm not really. I mean, I...," Kristy mumbled. "Well, I guess it's a tough field for a... I just... I don't know if I'm ready for it."

"Sure you are," said Robert. He could feel Kristy's heat. He could smell her stale sweat. "Teach those dumb boys a thing or two."

"We'll see about that. Maybe I should just go into teaching," said Kristy. "Um, did you need help with something?"

She slipped out from Robert's fervid gaze and started down the aisle. Robert followed her close behind.

"Oh yeah, I need some braided rope," he said.

"Yes, right over here," said Kristy, turning about-face and nearly bumping into Robert. "How much did you need?"

"Oh, one hundred and fifty feet should do it," Robert said, sliding up next Kristy as she pointed out the array of ropes in all colors hanging on the wall.

"Here, will this work?" she asked. Kristy pulled the loose end of a multi-colored, braided rope coiled up in a black spool. Robert leaned in close to Kristy, inspecting the rope in her hands. His chest pressed into her shoulder. Kristy made no attempt to pull away.

"Perfect," said Robert. He took the hefty lasso from her hands, brushing her fingers with his.

"I'll need to take it in the back to cut it to specifications. One hundred and fifty feet, right?" said Kristy.

"Yep, that'll do," said Robert.

"No prob. I'll bring it up to the counter for you," said Kristy.

"Cool," said Robert, backing off as Kristy pulled the spool from the wall.

"Here, I'll mark it down for you," said Kristy, heading down the aisle, roped bundled in her arms. "This stuff is way over-priced."

She fluttered her sparkling blues at Robert.

"You don't have to do that, really."

"No, no, no. Just take it," said Kristy. "It was nice to meet you, I'm sorry, I didn't get your name."

"Robert. And the pleasure was all mine, Kristy," said Robert. "Thank you very much. I guess. I guess I'll see you at the counter."

"Yep," Kristy called to him as he walked away, her sandy-blonde ponytail swishing as she hurried to the back of the store. "See ya at the counter."

Robert meandered about the store picking through the baseball mitts and footballs before finally making his way to the cash register. He lounged at the counter until Kristy hustled up with a hefty canvas bag, presumably filled with rappelling rope.

She gave Robert a shy smile and handed the bag to the middle-aged man with thick glasses who was ringing out the purchases. The balding man, perhaps the manager, or even the owner, gave Kristy a glare. She gave Robert a little wave and hustled back through the store. Robert watched her with interest until she disappeared into the aisles.

"Are you planning on doing some climbing?" the balding cashier asked Robert.

"Actually, yes," said Robert. "I did a little climbin' yesterday, just without the equipment."

"It's a good time of the year for it," said the cashier, perusing the receipt Kristy had slipped into the bag. "Not too hot, not too cold. Plus, the skeeters have all died out. This braid here is the best you'll find. It's strong all right. Where about you plannin' on goin'"

"I was thinkin' about going to Backbone," said Robert. "Figure I'll get in some fishin' while I'm at it."

The words dribbled out of his lips.

"It's pretty late in the season for trout," said the cashier, ringing up the order. He took Robert's money and replaced everything back inside the canvas bag. "We got some lures, though. I got this guy down in Missouri who ties them all hisself."

"That's alright," said Robert. "I really don't go fishing to catch fish."

"Say what?" said the cashier. He squinted at Robert, sucking on his buck teeth. "Well, good luck to you anyway."

"Yeah, thanks," said Robert. He picked up the bag and drifted away, leaving the store.

Clouds had blanketed the sun while Robert was inside. The ensuing chill forced him to a brisk pace. He entered a coffee shop on the corner of the block. The espresso options were listed on a blackboard behind the counter. In pink and green chalk someone had painstakingly calligraphed the menu. An acoustic folk song was piping through speakers strategically placed about the shop. A girl with a bowl haircut and coke-bottle glasses was manning the counter.

"Can I get anything for you?" she asked Robert.

"How about a coffee?"

"Cream or sugar?"

"No, black please."

"Dollar seventeen."

Change rattled on the table. Coffee was poured. Robert gingerly cradled the piping hot ceramic white cup with the pads of his fingertips. He weaved over to a sofa next to the front picture window. Robert sipped the steaming java, peering over the edge of the rim. He winced in pain and set the cup down as he spied Keith coming in through the door.

Keith saw Robert and gave a gleeful wave. He came over to the sofa.

"Hey Rob, what's up?"

"Hey Keith. Not much. How about yourself?"

Keith slung his book bag on the floor and nestled into an armchair across from Robert. He wore a backwards navy-blue Penn State cap, faded jeans, a Nike polo shirt, and Birkenstock sandals.

"Doin' all right. It's been a while."

"Yeah, graduation I think."

"Right, whatchya been up to? Last I heard you headed out to L.A. with Brett Cardell and Chad Hicks," said Keith. He flipped his hat around so that the bill hid his eyes.

"Actually, we went to New York," said Robert. He tested his coffee again.

"New York, no kidding. How was it?"

"I don't know. It just wasn't my thing, y'know. What've you been up to?"

"The whole school thing."

"Right. Are you gonna major in business?"

"I'm thinking about switching to computer science. That's where the money is, y'know," said Keith. "Hey, check out this hemp necklace I just bought."

Keith, with his hooked nose and brown hair curled up under the brim of his cap, revealed a beaded, twine necklace from under his collar.

"Nice," said Robert, slurping at his coffee.

They sat in silence for a moment.

"What do you have in the sack there?" Keith finally asked, pointing at the canvas bag at Robert's feet.

"Just some rope."

"Oh yeah? What's that for?"

"I was thinkin' about doing some serious climbing."

"You're finally going to climb that mountain?" asked Keith, his eyes shining with interest.

"Sure, why not? I got nothing better to do. See if God has a message for me."

Drops of mist began to condense on the windowpane of the café. A low rumble of thunder growled in the distance. Keith tapped his fingers on the armrest.

"So are you going to start school now?"

"Naw, doesn't really interest me."

"Really? I thought you had some writing scholarships lined up?"

"Yeah."

"I would think... I mean... Your grades were good enough, weren't they?"

"Yeah, I just sort of like don't belong."

"You gotta go to school man," gushed Keith excitedly. "There are so many parties, and the chicks. Man, you gotta go to school."

"Well, someday."

"Right, well I gotta get going," said Keith. "I have a ultimate frisbee game I gotta get to. I hope these clouds clear up. Take it easy."

"Yeah, nice seeing you."

"Later."

"Later."

Keith picked up his backpack and rushed out of the shop. Robert slowly sipped at his mug until it was empty and watched out the window as the raindrops became larger and more threatening. He glanced at his watch. He winced as he stood up. He stretched out his arms and sauntered out into the drizzle.

He reached into his pocket and pulled out a pack of cigarettes. He put one to his lips, and let it droop out of his mouth, unlit. A lady garbed in a black rain slicker rushed by with her umbrella hovered over her head, protecting her from the sprinkle. Robert returned the pack of smokes to his pocket and crammed his hands into them.

He wandered down the sidewalk for a few blocks, exiting the Crawford Falls downtown shopping district and into a residential neighborhood of turn-of-the-century brick-and-mortar Victorian houses. Rain collected in his shaggy, wavy, auburn hair and dripped down into his eyes.

He kept walking through town. Imported sedans and American-made pickup trucks whisked by, spraying the puddles in the air. Robert, soaked to the bone, crossed at a stoplight and entered a new residential development. The cookie-cutter houses were covered in matching white or beige plastic siding. He went down a cul-de-sac and stopped in front of a white-washed, two-story house with neat-trimmed grass and clipped hedges. Robert tossed his soggy, cigarette into a puddle and headed up the walk.

The sterile house was deserted. Robert roamed into the kitchen and opened the refrigerator. He peered into it blankly and then closed the door empty-handed. He trotted down the staircase into the basement. In a concrete room sat a weight set. His drum set was stacked in the corner.

Robert turned on a stereo and began to load weights onto the barbell. He sat on the bench for a moment, examined his palms, then stood up. He went back upstairs, went through the kitchen, and headed down a side hall. He entered a bedroom, which was supposed to be the guest room. For now it was Robert's room.

It was small, white, and sparse, furnished only with a single bed, a nightstand, and a desk. Robert sat down at the desk and opened a drawer. He rummaged through it and pulled out a pencil box. Inside were assorted pictures and scraps of paper. He laid down on his bed and gazed at each picture and poured over the notes intently.

There was a knock on his door.

"Robert, is that you?"

"Yes, Mom."

Robert hadn't heard her come home.

"Did you leave the radio on in the basement?" she asked.

"Yes, I guess so," said Robert. "Sorry."

"Please be sure to turn things off," hollered his mom through the closed the door. "Why don't you come help set the table, we'll be eating soon. I brought home pizza."

"Just a second," Robert said. He tossed the photographs and notes back into the box and shoved them into the drawer.

"What time did you get home?" Robert's mother asked as he sauntered into the kitchen. She was hunched over the stove, stirring some unseen vegetable poured from a can into the pot. She was wearing a navy-blue skirt and jacket accentuating her trim figure. Her makeup hid the few wrinkles that marred her striking face. Her silvery blonde locks were pulled back in a knot.

"Not too long ago," answered Robert.

"Did you have fun on your little trip?"

"Yeah, we had a good time."

Robert reached into the cupboard and took out a stack of plates.

"You look sick. Are you feeling well?"

"I'm fine."

"You should really get a job."

"I had one for a little while."

"I think you should get another one. Something that pays you good."

"Dad and I had this same discussion on Friday."

"Has your father called yet?"

"No."

"Do you know when he will be home?"

"No, I haven't talked to him."

Glasses clinked as Robert set four of them around the dinner table and filled them with milk from a plastic Hy-Vee jug.

"Why don't you call him and see when he is coming home."

"I'm sure he's on his way."

"Just call him," his mother huffed.

Outside, his father's Lincoln Continental pulled up the rain-spattered drive and parked in the garage. A door closed in the hallway and heavy feet stomped on the rug. Robert's father stood in the kitchen doorway, wearing a drenched overcoat and holding onto a black, leather briefcase.

"Well, I'm glad to see supper is ready and waiting for me," he sneered through his trim brown beard. Mr. Longley was a thick lumberjack of a man, the same height as Robert, only twice as wide.

"It will be ready in about ten minutes," his mother said tartly as she bustled about.

"When it's my turn to cook I always have supper ready at six whether anybody is here to eat it or not."

"Well, I'm sorry. I got held up by Dick just as I was ready to leave the office, so I was a little late getting home."

"Once in a while it would be nice to come home and have a nice, hot meal waiting for me," repeated Robert's father. He turned and disappeared from the kitchen.

"Robert, could you cut up some carrots for the salad, please?" asked his mother, her brow knitted.

"Yeah, sure thing."

Robert pulled a bag of baby carrots out of the fridge and placed a handful on a cutting board. He got a paring knife from the drawer and started hacking out small discs of carrot.

"I ran into Dale Campbell today," said his mother, stirring a can of mixed veggies into a pot.

Robert kept his eyes on his carrots.

"He asked how you were doing," his mother continued.

"Hm."

"He told me Melissa was going to Cornell."

"Yeah, she's a pretty smart girl."

"Have you talked to her recently?"

"No."

"Fine, I won't ask you any more questions. Will you go tell your father supper is ready?"

"All right."

Robert headed down the hallway. Light was creeping out from underneath the bathroom door. Robert lightly rapped on it.

"Dad, supper's ready."

"All right, just a second," his dad called back.

Robert walked back into the kitchen and sat at the dinner table. His mother set a tray of steaming French bread on the table and took her seat.

"Is your father coming?"

"Yeah, he's in the bathroom."

Robert began to fill his plate, and his mother did the same.

"Be sure to take some salad," she said.

"I really don't want any."

"Take some. You need vitamins. You've been eating too much junk lately."

"No, I'm fine. I just don't want any salad."

"Fine, but this is why you're so tired all the time. You don't eat good enough. You need fruits and vegetables to keep you going."

"Where's Jess at?"

"She's at cheerleading practice."

The chandelier hanging above the table chimed as a clap of thunder shook the house.

"I hope you aren't planning to go anywhere tonight," said Robert's mother. "The weather is supposed to be horrible."

"Don't worry, Mother. I'll be all right," groused Robert. He shoveled a spoonful of mixed vegetables into his mouth.

"The rain should be good for the grass," Robert's father said as he entered the dining room. He joined his family. Sitting at the head of the table he loaded a heaping slice of pizza onto his plate. "So, how was everyone's day?"

"Those people at work are driving me crazy," replied Robert's mother without pause. "Dick won't get off of my back about the Fillmore account and then Susan, you know Susan Dougherty, right? Well Susan doesn't have the figures done yet so I can't get anything finished. I tell you I am so sick of them."

"I keep telling you to find a new job."

"I know."

"What did you do today, Robert?"

"Not much."

"It's good to have you here."

Robert glared at his father's smirk.

"Did you find a job today?" his father asked.

"No."

"That new coffee shop is hiring."

"Yeah, I know. I was just there today."

"Did you pick up an application?"

"No."

"Are you going anywhere tonight?"

"I haven't decided yet."

"Where would you go?" his mother piped in.

"Probably go over to Eric's."

"Again? Didn't you just spend the last three days with him? What do you guys do all the time?"

"Just hang out."

"I'm not sure if I really trust those guys," his mother continued. "What's that boy's name? Ogre? Doesn't he have a nose ring?"

"Don't worry about it. They're good guys."

"Just be careful, all right," said his father as he looked up from his plate. "Whatever happened to Cody, Keith, and those guys?"

"I still see them every now and then."

"They were nice boys," Mrs. Longley chimed in.

"Yep," said Robert.

"Say, Robert, I'm going to the cabin on Saturday to fix some windows. I would really appreciate your help," said his father as he picked up his plate and took it to the sink. Robert did the same.

"What time're you going?" asked Robert.

"I'll probably leave around nine."

"I don't know. I'll have to see what's happening."

"It will only take a couple of hours. A little hard work wouldn't hurt you any. Whatever doesn't kill you only makes you stronger."

"Yeah, sure," said Robert, stuffing the last piece of pizza crust in his mouth.

"Well, excuse me," he said, mumbling through the pizza. "Thank you for dinner Mom."

Robert got up from the table and went to his room. He grabbed a red notebook and a black pen from his desk. He carried them out into the hallway and entered the spare bathroom. He locked the door.

***

"Robert, Robert! Are you all right in there?" His mother's muffled voice filtered through the door. Robert had lost track of time.

"Yeah, Mom. I'm fine." Robert sat down his notebook and pen on his lap and grabbed a wad of tissue.

"Well, you've been in there for a long time! Come help with the dishes!"

"Okay, just a second."

The toilet flushed and Robert came out. He stopped by his bedroom to set his notebook on his bed. He went to the kitchen where is father was already washing dishes in the sink. Robert grabbed a dripping pan from his father.

"You know, Rob, I've been reading and looking into things, and if I knew back when I was your age what I know now I would have a couple million dollars nested in the bank."

"Hm."

"You should be setting at least one hundred dollars a month into a trust fund or some mutual funds and by the time you are forty you will be able to retire."

"That would be nice."

"I know it's easy for you now to get by and not have to worry about the future, but you can't be nineteen forever. There will be a day when you will wish you had listened to me."

"I just barely turned nineteen."

Robert dried off the last plate and set it in the cupboard. Then he trudged down to the basement and instead of heading to the weight room turned into the dank den, a family leisure room with lush red carpeting and wood-paneled walls. Robert sat down in a big, leather easy chair and turned on the big screen TV. Upstairs, the front door slammed shut.

"I'm home!" chirped his sister. Footsteps bounced down the stairs and Jess appeared in the doorway of the den. She was wearing tight cut-offs and a tank top that revealed quite a bit of her delicate features. Her blonde hair, with red highlights, was pulled back in a ponytail.

"Hi Robert. Whatchya doin'?"

"Nothin'."

"Anybody call for me?"

"I don't think so."

"Darnit."

"Are you expecting someone to?"

"No," said Jess, and she bounced out of the room. Robert maintained his stare at the television. He was left in peace for a good half hour.

"Robert!" Jess called from upstairs.

"What?" he hollered back.

"Come here for a second!"

"What do you need?"

"I need you to help me with my algebra!"

"Just a second," Robert grumbled. Robert climbed out of his throne, wincing as his knees crackled. We wobbled upstairs and found his sister at the dinner table, her textbook and papers splayed out like war maps.

"What number are you on?"

"Forty-two."

"Let me see what you've tried so far."

Jessica handed him her paper and he studied it with a frown.

"I don't understand all of this stuff about functions," Jess whined.

"Yeah, it takes a while to get the hang of it. I don't know if I can explain it to you, but I can show it."

Robert picked up a pencil and scribbled down some symbols and numbers and letters.

"There," he said. "That should be the answer. Did you see what I did?"

"Yeah, I think so."

Just then the teardrop lights of the chandelier flickered off but blinked right back on. Robert left the dining room and walked to his bedroom. He turned on his stereo, and Pearl Jam filled his room. Yellow Ledbetter. He flopped on his bed and picked up a book from the floor.

"Robert!" his mother called as she opened the door. She turned the volume knob down on the stereo. "Do you know where the box of candles is?"

"Yeah, it's in Dad's workroom."

"Can you get it for me? We might need them in case the power goes out."

Robert's mother sat on the edge of the bed. She stroked Robert's straggly red hair.

"Yeah, just a second," said Robert. "I only have a few more pages."

"When are you going to get a haircut?"

"Uhh, never."

"What are you reading?"

"'Heart of Darkness.'"

"Is it good?"

"Uh huh."

"Was that a 'yes' or a 'no'?"

"Yes."

"Oh, well. I'll leave you alone now. Don't forget the candles."

"I won't."

As she was leaving, Robert's mother kicked the canvas bag on the floor.

"What did you get?" she asked and pulled the knot of rope out of the bag. "What's this for?"

"Mountain climbing."

"Where in the world are you going to go mountain climbing?"

"Colorado."

"Why would you go there?"

"'Cause that's where the mountains are."

"You don't need to be smart."

"Sorry," Robert said, his eyes glued to his book.

"Does your father know about this?"

"Uh huh."

"Was that a 'yes' or a 'no'?"

"No."

Robert looked up for the first time to glare at his mother. She sighed and dropped the rope to the floor. She softly closed the door as she left.

After reading the last two pages, Robert went to the basement to retrieve the box of candles from his father's workroom, which shared space with the weight set. On the way up he could hear his sister jabbering on the phone as he passed her door. He hauled the box upstairs where he met his father in the hallway.

"Here's the candles," said Robert.

"Thanks," Mr. Longley said as he took the box from his son. "Your mother tells me you are thinking about mountain climbing in Colorado."

"It's just an idea."

"Life isn't a game, son."

"Don't worry about it."

"Okay, well your mother and I are going to bed now, so can you try to keep your music down?"

"Okay."

"And don't forget to put the dog in her kennel."

"Okay, goodnight."

"Goodnight."

Robert walked to the door of his sister's room and rapped on it.

"What?" Jessica called out. Robert walked in to find her in her pajamas, painting her toenails.

"Did you figure out the rest of your homework?"

"I'll just have Mr. Peterson help me tomorrow."

"Yeah, he ain't too bad. Goodnight."

"Goodnight."

"Um, Jess."

"Yes?" she said, keeping her concentration on her shiny, red toes.

"Be careful."

"What? You're weird."

Robert smiled and closed the door as he made his exit. He went into the garage and exited through the back door to go to the backyard.

"Bandit! Come here girl!" A squat spotted blue heeler scurried out from under the porch.

"Did you get all wet?"

Bandit pounced at Robert's knees, shaking dog-soaked rain all over his shins. Robert scratched her drenched head. "Come on. Let's go to bed."

Bandit followed Robert into the garage and into her kennel. He latched the gate and returned to the backyard. Lightning streaked across the sky. He counted the seconds until he heard the resounding crash of thunder. Rain poured down Robert's hair, and his T-shirt clung to his well-cut chest.

Finally, he tore his eyes away from the sky and retreated into the house. His sopping shoes squished as he entered his bedroom. He sat at his desk and picked up the receiver of his telephone. He held it for a second, then quickly dialed a number. It rang four times until someone answered.

"Hello?" a woman's voice crackled. "Hello?"

Robert slipped the receiver back to its home. He wiped the hair from his eyes and sighed. He found his notebook and opened it up. He quickly read over one page then set it down. Rising from the bed, his eyes darted across his room.

He rummaged through his desk drawer and pulled out a pack of cigarettes. He slipped one between his lips. Robert returned the pack of smokes to the drawer and found a book of matches. Striking up a flame, he inhaled, and a puff of smoke escaped from his nose. He dropped the spent match into his metal garbage pail.

Slowly, Robert lifted his rope from the floor. The rope sifted through his hands. He tossed the rope back onto the floor. He peeled off his soaked T-shirt, then found himself standing in front of his mirror. It was a mirror that lured Amaterasu out of her cave. Robert sneered at his reflection. A tuft of red hair spurted from his chest.

"You think you're so tough?"

He slipped off his shoes, shorts, and boxers. He stood up straight, shoulders drawn back. Just like David, in every way. Reluctantly, Robert pulled some dry clothes out of his dresser. Blue Jeans, T-shirt, flannel. He grabbed his smokes and snuck out of his room. He crept through the kitchen and out the garage door. In the darkness, he could here Bandit rustling in her kennel. He flicked on the light switch. His mother's burgundy Honda Accord sat in front of him. Robert fingered the keys in his pocket.

"Should I go?"

3

LONG PAST GOODBYE

September 10, 1996

"H ey, man. You got some yay?"

The small passenger room in the RV was clouded with Marlboro and pot smoke. The beat-up trailer rumbled and rattled and shook and shivered down the quaky highway.

"I think I have a little bit left," said Troy. He reached into a bag at his feet and pulled out a translucent orange medicine capsule. He poured out a tiny pile of white powder on a cluttered vinyl table in the middle of the rear compartment. He started chopping up lines with an expired credit card.

"Good thing Hicks and Blanche are dunzo," Cardell mumbled. His own bloodshot eyes darted from the table to the guitar in his lap to Hicks drooling next to him back to the table down to his guitar to his fingers then his fingers were in his mouth gnawing at the nails.

Having no nail left to chew, Cardell fumbled at the strings of the acoustic guitar. Distraught, he tossed it across the tiny room, and it rang out in discord. All Hail Discordia!

"Careful, man," Troy slurred. then he dipped his head down and snorted. His coiled hair looked like it was covered in cobwebs. Something started to beep in Cardell's pocket. He jerked in surprise then pulled a black cartridge out of the front pocket of his jeans. He examined the pager.

"Shit, it's my parents," he groaned. "I don't wanna talk to 'em."

Cardell slumped back in the battered couch. The highway rumbled outside. He moved Hicks' foot and picked up a lighter from the floor.

"They're calling pretty late," said Troy. He was sitting, leaning forward, on an Army cot across from Cardell. He was stroking Blanche's jet-black hair, whose head was curled up in Troy's lap, dozing in his crotch. A pink streak draped over her black eyelids. Troy picked up a drumstick with his other hand and started tapping out a furious beat on the cot frame.

"It's only eleven in Iowa," said Cardell, blazing up his smoke.

"Where are we now?"

"I don't know. Somewhere outside Boston."

"Isn't it a little disconcerting that we never know where we really are?" said Troy in his gravelly voice.

Cardell chuckled.

"I think it's comforting," he said. "That way no one knows where we're hiding out. Never let 'em see you coming."

Cardell waved a knowing finger at Troy.

"Right, right," Troy said with a smile. "Hey man, can I spot a square off ya? I'm fresh out."

"Yeah, if I can get one of those lines." Cardell eyeballed the two neat streaks of white crystals on the table.

"I suppose."

Cardell tossed him a cigarette that bounced off Blanche's bare bicep. Cardell leaned over the table, nose to the grind. The familiar metallic taste reverberated off the roof of his throat. His nostrils flared. His sinuses singed. Fire. Stars. All colors! The queen would like you to eat her snatch now. And Jesus wants you to massage his nutsack. Cardell's beeper went off again.

"Shit."

He glanced at it, rubbing vigorously at his nose, and saw his parents' number flashing at him again.

"You want that last line?" Troy asked. He was pointing at the single row of powder on the table.

"No, I should call my folks."

"Nah, man. Major buzzkill. Call 'em tomorrow."

"No, this might be important."

"Suit yourself," said Troy. He leaned over and inhaled the last line of coke. He surged back and clutched the bridge of his nose. He shook his head and settled back against the rattling wall of the RV massaging his buck teeth.

Cardell nudged Hicks. He didn't respond. Cardell reached over to Hicks and grabbed his junk. A hand slapped Cardell's, and Hicks was glaring at him.

"Whatchya doin' man?" he grumbled.

"Just tryin' to wake you up," said Cardell, easing into the arm of the fabric couch.

"What for?"

"I need to use your cell phone."

"Who are you callin'?"

"My folks."

"No way, man."

"Why not?"

"That costs mucho dinero. Use Gene's."

Hicks laid his bleached blonde head back down on the other arm of the couch and closed his eyes.

Cardell stood up as far as he could without hitting his head on the roof of the RV and wobbled to the front of the compartment. He opened the small, plywood door that led to the cabin. Their manager, Gene, was driving.

"Gene, can I use your phone?"

"Yeah, no problem. It's in the bag on the floor there," said Gene. Keeping one hand on the oversized steering wheel, Gene pointed to a bag on the floor of the empty passenger seat. The yellow lines of the infinitesimal highway caught in the dim headlights blurred under the wheels of the chugging vehicle.

"Thanks, man."

Cardell leaned over the passenger seat and rummaged through Gene's backpack and found his flip phone.

"How's it going back there?" Gene asked.

"Fine. Everyone's pretty much passed out. How you doin'?"

"Good. I took some uppers, so I'll stay awake a few more hours."

"Where we going again?"

"Back to NYC. You guys play at Dungarees' tomorrow night."

"Cool. Well, goodnight."

"Yeah, peace out."

When Cardell returned to the compartment Hicks was sitting by himself, smoking a cigarette.

"Did Troy and Blanche go to bed?"

"Yeah."

"Looks like I get the cot again tonight."

"Per usual," nodded Hicks, his puffy eyes half closed.

Cardell sat down on the cot and turned on the cell phone. After dialing, it rang three times, and his mother answered.

"Hey, Mom. It's me.... Yeah, I got your beep. I figured it was something important.... No, I hadn't heard anything.... How is he doing?... What?... You're kidding.... Really.... Jesus. Yeah, wow. I never would have thought.... Is it all right if I call you tomorrow and talk about this? I just need to think right now.... Yeah. Thanks for calling. I love you, too. Goodbye."

Cardell turned the phone off and set it down on the smeared table.

"What's going on?" Hicks asked.

Cardell's face had lost all its color.

"Robert's dead," he said. The words barely escaped his lips.

"What?" Hicks asked, sitting up.

"He died in a car wreck last night. He's dead."

"What the fuck."

"Yeah, no shit."

"What happened? Do they know?"

"My mom just saw it on the news. She couldn't get a hold of his parents. She just knows he died in a car crash last night."

"Jesus. What the fuck was he doing?"

"I don't know. I don't know."

They reclined in their thrones and stared off into their own separate corners of the RV. The road hummed by outside and the only noise inside the RV was the occasional sniffle.

4

— • —

First Person

September 22, 1996

The sun was shining brighter than it ever had before. There were still puddles, scattered by Babe, leftover from the last three days of rain. The deluge had stripped the last remaining leaves off the bare trees looming in front of the Crawford Falls Lutheran church, an archaic citadel of brick and mortar. The church's facade was shrouded in ash trees and creeper vines. The steeple rose ominously among the fields and parking lots that spread out on the edge of town.

Cody was decked out in his Sunday best, walking between his parents through the vast church parking lot. A flock of girls in white dresses and black and brown cardigan sweaters were trooping into the church just ahead of him.

"Cody!" Justine wailed as she spotted him. She was wearing a thigh-length black dress with laces at the hem. "It's just so sad, I can't believe it!"

Justine collapsed into Cody's chest, and he squeezed her shoulder.

"I know, neither can I," he said.

"I just can't control myself. I haven't stopped crying since I heard!"

"Yeah, I'm still in shock."

"I just saw him at Slim's like two weeks ago. He looked so happy."

"It's been a while... it's tragic," murmured Cody.

"I know! I'm going to go see how Keith is doing."

Even though her cheeks were streaked, and her eyes were sore, Justine still radiated under the spotlight of the sun. Her silky, brown hair curled around her ears, two barrettes holding it back at the sides, keeping it from obstructing her button-nosed face.

"Yeah, he's around here somewhere," said Cody.

"I'll talk to ya later."

"Yeah, later."

They grasped hands, her small, tender fingers intertwined in his. After one more full-bodied hug, Justine joined her friends, and Cody followed his mother and father into the church. They sat in the second row along with the rest of his friends and their parents. The back of the wood pew curved in, pushing into Cody's spine, forcing him to sit up straight. He looked around the sanctuary. A crowd of sad, wandering eyes gazed back, some in packs, some standing alone in the corner. He recognized Eric Jimenez, his head bowed, his long greasy hair covering his face.

There were two that were conspicuously missing.

Everyone here was here for the same reason as Cody. They were searching for an answer. An answer that would never be understood. The eternal question. Why?

The reverend in his black robe and white sash rose to the podium. He appeared to tower over the congregation as he grimly surveyed those who had gathered before him.

"Who is that?" Cody's mom whispered.

"Some guy from Minnesota," his father, a gaunt man with regal peppered hair, whispered back. "A Methodist."

"Hm," Cody's mom grumbled.

Cody perused through the funeral pamphlet. It said the reverend was named Brewer. Cody had never seen him before.

"Please rise for the opening hymn." The reverend's voice was booming, deep, and reverent.

Cody stood, squinting at the lyrics printed in small-print on the church bulletin and joined the sea of black in a mournful, solemn version of "How Great Thou Art."

The wake, which Cody had attended half an hour earlier, did little to stir his sympathy. If anything, he was angry.

Robert was dead and nobody knew why. Cody wanted to know how he should feel about it. He should feel sad. Instead, he felt empty, like his heart got sucked into a wormhole.

Robert was Cody's first friend when he moved to Crawford Falls nearly a decade ago. Cody's father, an executive, was transferred from the suburbs of Houston to this city that was part college town part blue collar factory town.

There was a clear divide among the students in school, and which side you fell upon depended on which church you attended. Cody's mother, a plump southern belle of proper upbringing, was damn sure that her family joined the stoic Lutheran society.

It was at his first Lutheran confirmation class that Cody met Robert. Keith and Little John and the other guys were also there, but they already had their own clique and weren't about to welcome a rich kid from Texas with open arms.

Robert stood out from the others. Not only because he knew the Bible verses better than everyone, but because he openly questioned the confirmation teacher, a boring housewife with a Mennonite-length dress, high-collar, and straw-like blonde hair who believed the best way to heaven was through oyster crackers and whole milk.

The lady splayed magazines all over the table. She had circled the ads with marker, highlighting the subliminal penises and boobs corrupting the minds of youth. While teaching about Zaccheus and his climb up the Sycamore tree she haughtily told the teenagers that money lenders were also godly people.

"Like Charles Keating?" Robert had blurted out.

The teacher was perplexed.

"Pornography is bad," Robert had chided, "but it's OK to steal three billion dollars from the trusting masses? Or did we already forgive and forget?"

Then there was the time they were forced to attend Bible camp, or else fail confirmation. Thanks to Robert's heroics, the Lutherans defeated the Baptist team handedly at volleyball. The Baptist leader, a farm boy from a family commune that worshipped guns and Jesus, told Robert he would pray for him.

Robert retorted, "You do know that Jesus was the first Jewish magician?"

The boy, with a black bowl cut and wandering eye, glared bloodily at Robert with his good eye.

"It breaks my heart that you're going to burn in hell," the boy growled.

Robert had laughed and strutted off, making sure to kick sand in the Baptist team's direction.

Robert and his parents had to meet with the Lutheran minister after that one. Robert was on the football team, and like everything else, it was swept under the rug.

Cody wanted Robert's funeral to be over. He wanted life to be normal. It would never be again. The party's over.

The viewing had been held in a side room next to the church sanctuary. Mr. Longley had given a little stirring speech, about how his family appreciated the help and support received from everyone and how they couldn't have gotten past this ordeal without it. Jess sang "Amazing Grace" in her warbling voice and the local Lutheran minister preached how the Lord shelters all of his sheep no matter how far they stray from the flock.

The cosmetologist had painted Robert's face, his chiseled cheekbones accentuated with a smattering of blush. It was surprising, considering the mangled hunk of steel his car was, that Robert's face didn't have a single blemish. Apparently, he was thrown through the windshield. All his injuries were internal. Robert always did brag about how hard his head was.

He was dressed in a suit that Cody knew Robert had never worn. Cody just wished he could look into Robert's eyes one last time and see that confidence, arrogance. No fear. The last time Cody saw Robert, at some kegger in the woods, Robert was withdrawn, hiding in the dark recesses of the trees, his eyes glassy, his skin pale, like an AIDS victim rubbing away the track marks.

Color scorched Cody's cheeks. He tore his eyes away from Robert's corpse and he walked away from him one last time.

"...as we walk through the valley of the shadow of death..."

The Methodist preacher interrupted Cody from his muse. It was at least the third time he had bellowed the phrase with the appropriate amount of bravado, sorrow, and aplomb.

***

As Cody had walked away from the casket, he saw Melissa Campbell sitting on a wooden chair with a worn felt seat. She was dabbing at her eyes while her boyfriend comforted her. Cody passed them without a word.

At the church cafeteria he found his friends at a folding table throwing playing cards back and forth.

"Full house boys! Time to pay the piper!" shouted Mike boisterously. He chuckled and collected his winnings. His tie squeezed out three more chins on his flabby neck.

"We got time for another hand?" asked Cody, dragging over a folding chair from the next table.

"Yeah, we got like ten minutes," said Keith, shuffling the cards in an arc.

"What're the rules?" Cody asked as he sat between Little John and Kiljoy. Little John's shoulders were bursting out of his jacket. Kiljoy was drowning in his oversized suit, his pointy nose making him look like a pasty penguin.

"Suicide kings and one-eyed jacks," called out Keith as he distributed the cards. Keith looked as sharp as ever, his hair slicked in a wave, his black tie snug under his starched collar.

"Deal me in," said Cody.

***

"...and lead us not into temptation but deliver us from evil..."

Cody glanced at his mother. Her eyes were moist. Her makeup glowed like a televangelist's second wife. She gave him a warm smile as she gripped his hand.

***

"You know what song they should play?" Little John asked at the poker table while interrogating his cards.

"Give me three," said Cody. He laid down the said number of cards. "What song's that?"

"That Nick Cave song Robert was always playing."

"Right."

"They should play Metallica," said Kiljoy, laying down all five of his cards in surrender. "Metallica kicks ass."

"Rob would have hated that."

They all snickered in agreement.

"I can't believe some of the people that showed up," Mike added.

"Right. Like Debi Harris and all her friends. They didn't know we never existed. What were they, seniors our sophomore year?" Keith noted.

"Everybody knows Rob," said Little John, silencing them all.

"Rob would have hated this whole thing. Hell, it's sacrilegious enough holding the funeral in a church."

***

"...I was hungry, and you fed me, thirsty and you gave me a drink..."
Cody shuffled in his pew and stifled a yawn.

***

"You boys put those cards away this instant!" A little white-haired lady was hovering over their table, her fists shaking. "This is no way to honor the dead!"

"We weren't..." started Kiljoy.

"I can't believe you boys! Gambling in a church. Didn't your parents teach you any respect?"

"Sorry, we'll quit," mumbled Cody as he set down his hand.

"You boys pay some respect. This is not an occasion for games. You should learn some manners...," shrieked the lady. She continued to grouse as she stalked away from the table.

"Jesus, she had a hair up her ass."

"No shit. Her panties sure are bunched up."

"What's it her business anyway? We aren't even using money."

"Dumb bitch."

"This sucks. I had a full house."

***

"...Would the pallbearers Michael Ahrendson, Cody Gordon, Allen Kiljoy, Keith Johnson, and John Williams please come forward?"

The five boys, now men, rose together, like thrift store druids, and shuffled to the front of the sanctuary. They each grabbed hold of the brass rail on Robert's closed casket. All in step, they slowly proceeded out of the church. A couple of older guys directed them to a sleek black hearse. Soon, a stream of suits and dresses poured out of the church.

***

"Shotgun!" shouted Keith as he ran for Little John's station wagon. They all piled into the blue beast, splotched with rust and off-color makeovers. Cody, Mike, and Kiljoy sat in the middle bench in respective order.

"I hate ties," grumbled Mike as he slipped the knot down and pulled his tie over his head. The engine spluttered a few times as Little John cranked the ignition. It finally turned over and he revved the gas. They pulled out from the church parking lot and followed Roberts' parents' Ford F-150.

"Check out what I got," said Keith as he pulled a package out of his jacket pocket.

"Cool, cigars," Kiljoy chirped. "Give me one."

"Chill out," shouted Mike, who punched Kiljoy in the arm.

"Are those Swishers?" Little John asked in his deep baritone.

"You got a lighter?" Cody asked. He took the package of Swisher Sweets from Keith and pulled off the wrapper.

"Shit, I forgot."

John popped in the lighter on the dashboard. Soon, cigars were lighted, and smoke poured out of every window.

"Put on some tunes!" called out Mike. Kiljoy hacked out a cloud of smoke.

"You're not supposed to inhale, dumbass."

"I know," Kiljoy gagged.

"Put in something cool," Cody called out.

"You'll like this. I have just the thing," said Little John as he slid a CD into the changer and cranked up the volume. The first distorted chords of "Smells Like Teen Spirit" twanged through the speakers and cheers erupted from all five mouths. Conversation ceased and became a chorus of unintelligible howling and headbanging for the rest of the parade.

Once at the cemetery, the five boys once again carried the coffin. The coffin was lopsided, angling up where Little John carried one corner by himself. A garden of flowers surrounded the gaping hole in the earth. They all sat in the front row in folding chairs next to Robert's father, mother, and sister. The sun still glared down on them. Each of the five boys dawned a pair of Oakley sunglasses.

"...Let us all bow our heads in prayer..."

Sobs and sniffles could be heard scattered around them. Robert's mother and sister covered their faces with lacy handkerchiefs and his father trembled noticeably.

"...as we walk through the valley in the shadow of death..."

Cody slouched down a bit in his chair. He checked his watch. 4:17. He folded his arms and watched Mike play with his tie, which was back around his neck. A bead of sweat dripped down Cody's forehead and he wiped it away.

"...baptized in the name of the Father, the Son, and the Holy Spirit..."

Cody sat up straight. He turned and looked at all the faces. He looked at his parents, his mother crying into his father's shoulder. He saw old men and women he had never met. He saw all his friends from school. There were kids he had never seen before. There were so many people he did not know. How well did these people really know Robert? Who really knew Robert? Yet here they all were. Cody turned back around and faced the Methodist minister from Minnesota.

"...Ashes to ashes, dust to dust..."

Slowly, painfully, the casket lowered into the hole.

The crowd began to disperse in small groups. Each a huddled mass holding onto each other for support.

Cody's mother came up and hugged him.

"I'm so sorry," she whispered.

"It's all right, Mom."

"Are you going to come with us?"

"I think I'm going to ride home with the guys, if that's all right."

"Yes, that's fine. Just be sure to be home for dinner."

"Yeah, sure thing."

He watched his parents leave in their new Cadillac. Mrs. Longley walked up to him and embraced him. She looked older. She smelled like soap.

"Thank you," she sobbed. "I'm sorry I'm like this. I don't mean..."

"It's all right," said Cody. He embraced her back. She found all five boys and gave them each a hug, followed by her husband.

"You guys are really great," said Rob's father. "Robert was lucky to have friends like you."

"Thanks."

Mr. and Mrs. Longley held each other and slowly marched to their truck, followed by their forlorn daughter, Jessica.

Soon everyone was gone. Cody, Keith, Mike, Kiljoy, and Little John stood in a circle around the astroturf blanketing the burial spot. A brown, marble gravestone shone proudly in the sun.

Robert Joseph Longley

B. August 30, 1977

D. September 9, 1996

Lord, to whom shall we go?

You have the words of eternal life.

John 6:68

A tear rolled down Cody's cheek, and he wiped it away.

5

Sweet Kansas City Jazz

September 2, 1994

The Crawford Falls High School football field spread out before Robert like a green bed of confetti. The football field was his playground. His heart was giddy. His knees were light and bouncy. His vision heightened. It was time to play.

Robert stood poised at the line of scrimmage, his hands hung limp at his side, his eyes glued to Keith.

"Hut!" Keith the quarterback bellowed, his hands nestled under the center. Robert's breath thundered inside his helmet. Through the crossbar he glanced at the cornerback lined up across from him. Their eyes locked and burned. Show this bastard no mercy. Take no prisoners. There were only fifteen seconds on the scoreboard, now fourteen. This is it, no timeouts, and four points behind. Coach Martin screamed orders from the sideline.

"Hold your blocks!" No one gets by! Let's go, let's go!"

Robert gave his hands a shake. His shoulders shivered and he let out a sigh. Keep still, stay calm. Everybody on the field was a Greek statue, molded with energy and anticipation. A panorama of enemies at war. This was the final strike, the last chance for victory in a bloody, ruthless battle.

Little John, the starting left tackle, bent his knee backwards in the third quarter. Now Kenny the towering halfwit from the special ed class was guarding

Keith's blindside. As a result, Robert, a wide receiver who was meant to zig, zag, and juke was chip-blocking linebackers. With the game on the line and forty yards to the end zone, Coach Martin had no choice but to let Keith let the ball rip.

Man against man, muscle against muscle, steel against steel. Robert's white uniform was streaked with grass stains and smeared with dirt. His face was a sweaty mess. His legs were aching from the constant attack.

"Hut!" Keith wailed. This is it. No stopping now. There's one last hand to be dealt. Don't blink. Don't flinch. Keep the wheels turning. No time for doubts or second guesses. There are four white hashmarks between here to victory. And now there's only eight seconds to cover the distance.

"Hut!"

Robert took off.

His burning legs churned over the battered grass. His arms pumped with gridiron determination. His heart pounded and the defender nipped at his heels, slapping at his wrist. Robert streaked down the sideline, his teammates screaming at him, but they were only wind.

Robert turned his head to see the ball spiraling toward him. He gnashed his teeth and pushed harder. He was oblivious to his screeching muscles, his wasted lungs, and the enemy soldier hunting him down. The ball was a missile, sailing closer and closer. He strained his body, gaining two steps on the defender. Robert stretched his arms out as the ball flew over his shoulder. The ball dropped in his waiting hands. It stuck to his fingers, and he tucked it tightly under his bicep.

Robert strode into the end zone, his arms raised victoriously. His eyes blazed with fury, and he rang out a feral battle cry. Cheers engulfed him from every side. The crowd was on its feet. The cheerleaders were dancing. The coach was leaping on the sideline. His teammates hoisted Robert on their shoulders. Robert pointed to the sky, his face overcome with elation. The clock was stopped at zero. He felt no pain. All the weariness inside him had drained. Robert dropped to the ground and embraced Keith.

"We did it!" he cried.

One more battle down. One more notch in his hammer. There would be no tears tonight, only celebration. Only winners take home the glory, and only heroes show up to battle the next day.

Who's the rock star? What more can you ask for?

6

CAN SOMEONE CATCH DEAN?

August 19, 1996

Reverend Brewer considered Highway 218 to be a blessing. "The Avenue of the Saints." It made his trip from Minneapolis to St. Louis, and back again, like a Sunday drive. He was helping to lead seminars on how to reach inner-city youth and made the trip every month. More so now that things were heating up. Still, during so many of these trips home, he couldn't fight the nagging feeling that this convention hall of preachers never actually got anything accomplished. When you get so many preachers under the same roof, nothing but empty promises, flowery sermons, and limp handshakes.

At least Reverend Brewer had put in enough years to finally start earning some respect among the order. Was he as arrogant as some of the younger pastors? Like Reverend Johnson from Kansas City. The man would not give up. Like a little terrier, yapping and carrying on. Lord, the way he orates, you would think we need to take up arms against the gays and abortionists. Apocalypse my ass. The Lord works in his subtle ways. And all are God's children.

Reverend Brewer wasn't a flamboyant minister. He wasn't overpowering or overbearing. He was stoic and humble. Preaching straight from Psalms and the New Testament. He was a big man, not large, just solid. He commanded the pulpit, with his strong features, sharp nose, black-framed spectacles, and jutting chin. His resounding voice reverberated off the stain-glassed windows. His love for God emanated from his whole being.

More importantly were his visits to the nursing homes to spend time with bedridden old folks who hadn't seen their grandkids in years. Every Thursday he helped deliver the Meals on Wheels to invalids whose wrecked bowels didn't allow them to leave home. On Wednesdays he hosted a pizza party at the youth home.

Reverend Brewer wasn't as interested in talking about Jesus as he was in conducting service in the name of Jesus. It was what he learned from his father, a Methodist minister from Chicago.

Be the hen who lays the egg, not the rooster crowing his fool head off.

Reverend Brewer had only just started for home and was fifteen minutes outside of St. Louis when he sped past a young man thumbing for a ride at the side of the highway. How could he be wearing jeans and a flannel shirt on such a scorching summer day? He must be burning up.

Reverend Brewer slowed to a stop on the side of the road and backed up his '92 Camry along the shoulder. The young man loped up to his passenger window, a green Army duffel bag weighing him down. The Reverend lowered the passenger side window, and the hitcher leaned in.

The man had boyish features, with a splotchy red beard covering his gaunt cheeks. He couldn't be more than eighteen, but those worn, drained striking blue eyes belonged on the face of a war veteran. He had windblown red hair that swirled around his head.

Where you headed?" the Reverend asked.

"CF... um... Crawford Falls, Iowa."

"I can take you to Des Moines."

"Perfect."

"You can just toss your bag in the back seat."

The man did so, and he slammed the passenger door as he got in the car. He sank into the passenger seat with a sigh and fastened his seatbelt.

"My name's Robert Longley," said the man, glancing sideways at Reverend Brewer.

"I'm Reverend Joseph Brewer," the Reverend said. He took Robert's hand in his and shook. The Reverend almost winced at the strength of the man's vice-like grip.

Reverend Brewer looked behind his shoulder to check for traffic and eased back out onto the highway. He punched the accelerator, and the Camry lurched ahead.

After a few minutes of silence as the Midwest landscape whooshed by in hues of green and blue, with the occasional cow, Reverend Brewer finally said, "You know, what you're doing could be dangerous. Hitchhiking, y'know."

Robert was slouched down in the passenger seat, his elbow perched on the door, his cheek resting on his fist. He turned his head to look at Reverend Brewer, then looked back out the window.

"Yeah, I know," said Robert. "But there's nothing else to do. I'm stranded... in goddamn Missouri."

"Missouri's about the worse place to be stranded," chuckled Reverend Brewer. "Like Elijah in Beersheba."

"Take my life," mumbled Robert. "I am no better than my ancestors."

Reverend Brewer gave Robert a long look with a slight smirk.

"Get up, and eat!" bellowed Reverend Brewer, with a dramatic shake of his fist. "If you do not you will not be strong enough for the long trip!"

Robert chuckled.

"So you know Kings," laughed Reverend Brewer.

"More than I'd wish," said Robert, shaking his head.

"Well, if you reach in the back seat there, in my backpack, there's a couple of granola bars," said Reverend Brewer, motioning toward the backseat. "They're in the front pocket. Grab one for me, will ya? And one for yourself."

Robert reached back and rummaged through the said backpack until he sat up straight again with two granola bars in his mitts. He handed one to Reverend Brewer and unwrapped one for himself. They quietly munched away.

"Robert," said Reverend Brewer, finally. "Why are you here?"

"The Israelites broke their promise," mumbled Robert through a mouthful of granola. "I guess it's time to go climb a mountain."

"It seems God found you at the right time," said Reverend Brewer. "Perhaps you need to go home, kiss your mother and father, then find your Mount Horeb."

"Maybe you're right," said Robert.

Crumbs of granola dropped on his flannel shirt. Robert brushed them off.

"Elijah was kinda a bitch," added Robert. "Wasn't he."

7

—— • ——

LOVE BLOOD GREED SEX DEATH BIRTH

September 3, 1994

A typical Saturday night in Crawford Falls took place in the basement of Cody's upper-class residence where the lush carpet smelled of shampoo and the mildew was smothered with latex paint. On this particular Saturday night Cody's dad was away on business per usual and his mother was busy fretting away upstairs in the kitchen, every once in a while politely calling from the top of the basement stairs to see if anyone wanted pop or pizza bites.

The five teenage boys were circled around a card table in the basement. Cody dealt three cards each to himself, Keith, Little John, Kiljoy, and Mike. Soda cans and potato chips were scattered all over the room and MTV was on the tube television playing a Metallica video.

"This song kicks ass," said Little John. He grabbed a remote and blared the volume.

"The *Black* album is awesome," said Mike, as he hollered over "Enter Sandman."

"*Master of Puppets* is the best," Little John yelled back.

"What about *...And Justice For All*?" Kiljoy asked.

"You just like it cuz of 'One,'" said Mike, and he slugged Kiljoy in the shoulder.

"Ouch. I do not, you bitch," griped Kiljoy, and he hit Mike back. The two toppled over backwards in their folding chairs and tumbled to the soft floor partaking in a rousing bout of fisticuffs.

Finished, they laid panting on the floor, bellies exposed under their gray CF Tigers sweatshirts. Cody heard his mother's footsteps frantically scurry across the floor upstairs. The basement door creeped open, and she called out, "Is everything all right down there?"

"Yes, Mom!" hollered Cody, his baby face, peppered with pimples like polka-dots, was scrunched in a scowl.

"Okay!" called out his mom. "Let me know if you need anything."

She quietly ushered the door shut. The teenage boys, with Mike and Kiljoy retaking their seats at the table, perused their cards.

"Where the hell is Rob? It's almost ten," groused Keith as he discarded a two of spades.

"You know him," snickered Mike. "He stopped to look in a mirror."

"Yeah," said Kiljoy. "He's still doing his hair."

"He got his mom's old car today," said Cody as he laid down the queen of hearts. "He's probably cruisin' around."

"Sweet, I needed that," said Little John, and he swiped up the queen. "His mom's Civic? He got it for his birthday, right?"

"Yeah," said Mike, his round face, squashed like a bulldog, was flushed and sweaty. "If I was him, I'd take it to the shop, suspend the shocks, lower the chassis."

"Fuck yeah, tint the windows, pimp it out," said Kiljoy, his thick spectacles cocked sideways, his straw-like hair sticking up at the cowlick.

"Is it all right if I put in a CD?" asked Cody. He stood up and hunched over the stack stereo next to the TV.

"What are you putting in?" asked Little John.

"Juliana Hatfield."

"Instead of Metallica?"

"The video's almost over," said Cody as he hit play on the stereo. He leaned over and hit the power button on the TV. It flickered off. He took his seat and picked up his hand.

"Whose turn is it?" he asked.

"Yours," Mike answered. Footsteps thumped down the carpeted basement stairs, and Robert burst into the room.

"What's up, fellas?" He had on a high school football T-shirt and faded corduroys hanging off his lithe frame. His long floppy hair curled at his ears.

"Hey there sweet tits," said Keith, who kept his brown hair shaved high and tight. "How's freedom?"

"I couldn't stop the car, dude. I was ready to drive to Omaha," Robert giggled, as he collapsed on a lumpy, overstuffed couch in the corner of the room.

"You got the Civic?" Little John asked as he wrapped his meaty knuckles on the table. "I'm knockin'."

"You shithead!" cursed Kiljoy and he slapped his hands on the table, disturbing the discarded cards.

"You guys playin' thirty-one?" asked Robert, craning his neck and checking out the game. "Nice hand, Little J."

Then he gave a big, shit-eating grin.

"Yeah, man," Robert continued. The Civic's all mine. Dad's gonna buy my mom a new Accord."

"That's not a bad deal."

"Yeah, and since I got an A-plus in calc, they're paying for my insurance, too," said Robert, stuffing a handful of chips in his mouth.

"What a rip-off! You totally failed calc!" Mike burst.

"I've got connections," Robert mumbled, spraying bits of chips.

"Just because Coach Martin is your teacher," said Little John, laying down his three cards. "Thirty."

The other four laid down their hands following in order.

"I hate this game! I always lose!" shouted Kiljoy, slamming a nickel in the pot.

Robert got up off the couch and went to the stereo, dragging his backpack with him. He hit stop on the CD changer and replaced Juliana Hatfield with the

Weezer *Blue* album. With "My Name is Jonas" blaring in the speakers, Robert squeezed a sixth folding chair between John and Cody at the table. He slapped Little John on the thigh.

"How's the knee?" Robert asked John.

"Sore as hell," said Little John with a grimace. "But I'll live."

"You okay to play next week?" asked Robert. "We're at Bishop."

"I'll glue it on if I have to," grumbled Little John. He had the same mop-top haircut as Robert, only blonde and half as long.

"We're in trouble if you can't suit up," said Keith, looking at Little John wide-eyed.

"Yeah," giggled Mike. "No way is Robert gonna make that Hail Mary catch again."

"No shit," laughed Robert.

"That's our first play on Friday," said Keith, with a chuckle. "I'm gonna audible outta whatever run Martin calls."

"You gotta let Klink run all over Bishop," said Mike serious as a heart attack. "That's the only way we'll win."

"That buttmunch can suck my nuts," laughed Robert, swatting his crotch with the back of his hand.

"You know he's sucking Martin's nuts," grumbled Little John.

The five boys burst in laughter, tipping back in their chairs.

"Let's play for some real money," said Robert, when the din had died down. "How about poker?"

"I don't know how to play," said Kiljoy, handing his cards to Robert so he could shuffle.

"You don't know how to play poker?"

"I've never played before, so sue me."

"All right, you try to get two, three, or four of a kind, or a straight. A straight is like two, three, four, five, six. A full house is if you have three of a kind and a pair at the same time. A flush is if all five cards are the same suit, order doesn't matter. You can learn as we play. The game is five card stud, gentlemen, what you see is what you get."

"You can learn as we take your money," sneered Mike, jabbing Kiljoy in the ribs.

The cards arced in a flurried bridge, and Robert slid five cards to each of his friends.

"A quarter to ante, a five-dollar limit per round, and the suicide king and one-eyed jacks are wild."

"What are the suicide king and one-eyed jacks?" asked Keith, picking up his hand.

"The king of hearts and the jack of hearts and spades," said Robert. "Who hasn't anted?"

"Oh, me," said Little John, tossing in a quarter.

"What's the game plan tonight?" asked Robert as he sorted through his hand.

"You're lookin' at it," Cody answered.

"We did that last night," said Robert, slurping at a can of Coke. "What's your bet?"

"Twenty-five cents," said Mike, pondering his cards.

"Come on pussy, I raise you a buck," Little John said, slipping a dollar bill underneath his quarter. "Hey Keith, isn't your cousin having some friends over tonight?"

"Yeah, she pretty much does every night," Keith said. "I see your bet, and I'm gonna raise it another fifty cents."

"Who's gonna be there?" asked Robert.

"Shit, I gotta fold," said Cody, laying down his hand.

"Y'know, probably Rachel, Melissa, Justine, maybe some others."

"What're we doin' here? Let's get in my Civic and roll," said Robert. He threw his cards down and stood up.

"You just wanna get in Melissa's pants," Little John laughed.

"So, they're some pretty good pants, y'know what I mean."

"Hell yeah! So are Justine's," shouted Little John, standing up too.

"I don't know. My parents want me home by eleven. We were out late last night," said Keith, remaining seated, ruminating over his cards, his bushy eyebrows angled down toward his hooked nose.

"What are you talking about? We had a game last night. We won for shit's sake. And you won it for us!" said Robert, shaking his shaggy head. "Dude, It's Saturday night! What have you got to do tomorrow?"

"I got church in the morning."

"Jesus Christ! That's the lamest excuse I ever heard. There is a house full of chicks just sitting there unattended. This could possibly be the greatest night of our lives!"

"Yeah! Chicks! I'm goin'!" Kiljoy chimed in.

"Let me call my folks," said Keith. He retrieved a cordless phone from the side table next to the couch and dialed.

"Dammit," said Mike, slapping down his cards. "I had two pair."

***

Soon, they were all piled into the tiny, blue Honda Civic, Robert and Cody up front, the other four squeezed in the back seat like a bunch of clowns. Little John took up half of the seat. Keith was squished into the window. In the middle, dwarf-like Kiljoy sat halfway on Mike's lap.

"Shouldn't we have called first?" asked Keith.

"No way, man," said Robert as he accelerated through a yellow light. "Never let 'em see you comin'. I mean, maybe we'll catch them in their nighties."

"Yeah, cool!" Kiljoy agreed whole-heartedly, as he wiggled his elbow free from Mike's ribs.

"Check out what I got," said Robert. He leaned over and opened the glove compartment. He jerked up as the car swerved and steadied the wheel.

"Can you get those for me?" he asked Cody.

"What am I looking for?"

"You'll know when you see them."

"These?" asked Cody, pulling out a package of cigars.

"You got it. There should be another pack in there."

"Cool! Are those Swisher Sweets?" asked Little John, snagging the package out of Cody's hand.

"Yeah dude," said Robert. "Here's a lighter. Roll down the windows, will ya?"

John took the yellow lighter from Robert, ripped open the package, and one by one, four cigars blazed up in the back seat.

"Here you go, dude," said Robert, holding out a cigar for Cody.

"No thanks, man," said Cody, holding his palm up like a stop sign. "That's not my thing."

"That's cool," said Robert, tucking the stogie back into the pack. He tossed the pack onto the dashboard. "You guys want to hear some Zeppelin?"

"Yeah!" said Mike, barely making a sound before gagging out a cloud of smoke and bursting into a tirade of coughing.

"You're not supposed to inhale these things, you'll kill yourself," said Robert, rummaging through his tapes and pulling out a cassette. He popped it in the car stereo. "A Whole Lotta Love" blasted through the factory speakers.

"We should have a jam session tomorrow!" bellowed Robert over the music.

"Yeah, I'll bring my guitar over!" Cody yelled back.

"How about you guys?"

"What?"

"We should jam tomorrow!" Robert's voice cracked under the pressure he was putting on his vocal cords.

"Sure!" Little John replied.

"I can't make it!" Keith called.

"What?"

"I can't make it!" Keith cupped his hands over his mouth.

"Can I use your dad's guitar?" Kiljoy screeched.

"I'll have to ask him!" Robert yelled back.

They headbanged without any conversation until they pulled up in front of a yellow, vinyl-sided ranch house shrouded in the dark shadows of elm trees and juniper shrubbery.

"This is it boys," said Robert. He pulled the key out of the ignition. The six teenage boys piled out of the car and weaved up the driveway.

8

A Dream

A foul beast lies dormant inside, bubbling, and brooding for a time when it can free its scaly head from its symbiotic confinement. Freedom to reign will be his again. Terrorizing the countryside in its hopeless search for satiety. Raping maidens of their leather pride, chewing their souls, and leaving their garters flapping in the wind.

Is there no shining white knight to slay it? Where is Sir Lancelot when you need him? Have all heroes atrophied? Basking in a sun ray dropped upon the earth by the consequential stairwell spiraling down; or is it up? Is it easier to step down, or step up? It is easier to feed the beast than it is to strike it down.

Only the weak pray. Crooked cords of discontent attributed to a lyre that has not been strung. Distorted words and broken spines, chained gods and lashed saints, cured the disease by feeding the beast.

Only the ghosts speak the truth, that is why we fear them so. Clouds loom over the horizon. A breeze is stirring the sea. The beast will soon rise. Who will your savior be?

9

HOLIDAY THIEVES MARKET

September 3, 1994

Was that really my finger pressing the doorbell?

If I was here by myself, I could have easily hesitated. I could have slunk away in the night. Never seen. Never here. Just another shadow created by the moonlight.

Instead, with five peers hovering behind me I pressed ahead and rang the bell before I could have second thoughts. Like jumping off the high dive. We made the leap now we have to deal with the consequences.

Behind me, Mike and Kiljoy were giggling nervously. Little John was grinning, but he was cool. Keith was scowling, and Cody was gazing off in mild annoyance. Fuck 'em. This night was mine. They were here because I brought them here. This was what being a rock star was all about.

But what was I going to do if someone answered the door. Maybe no one would answer, and I could leave with my pride intact. But all the lights were on. There was movement inside. Melissa was inside. I looked back at the boys. No turning back. Shake it off. Shake it off. She's as scared of you as you are of her.

"Chicks, dude," Kiljoy relished. I jumped when the door handle turned, and the entrance swung open.

"Oh, hey guys." Keith's cousin, Robyn, gave us a crooked, metal smile. "What's going on?"

I took a quick glance behind me. Stares of fire blazed at me. Expressionless faces of pure teenage angst and agony pushing me forward. This was my cue.

"Uh, not much. We were just cruisin' around."

Beautiful. Aloof. Vague, but got the point across. Still, I was breathing harder than I would have liked. Why is my nose stuffed? God don't start dripping snot.

"What are you up to?" I continued, setting my volley, fighting the urge to wipe my nose.

"Nothing really," said Robyn, tilting her head, her dark bangs curled like chrysanthemum. "We're just hanging out."

No eye contact. Very cool. A professional.

"Oh yeah?" I asked. There was dead silence behind me. They expected me to blow this. I could feel it. I'll show 'em. "Who's here?"

"Just us girls. Justine, Rachel... and Melissa."

What was that pause? A hidden message?

"Do you mind if we stop in?" I asked. I couldn't believe I just said that. What if she says no? "We got, like, a eighteen-pack a Mountain Dew bottles. Like, if we drink 'em all by ourselves, um, y'know, we'll be wired 'til Christmas."

"And Nilla Wafers," Kiljoy added. Fuck. Shut up you idiot. You'll blow our cover.

"My parents aren't home..."

"Who's there?" a voice sang from the other room. Justine. Sweet, we're in. Robyn opened the door wider and stepped aside. She turned her head and called back to Justine.

"It's Keith and his friends."

"Oh, yay!"

Good ol' Justine. She does love the boys. In a heartbeat, her lovely face was squeezing through the door. Too much makeup, but not done in vain.

"What's goin' on guys?" Justine was glowing under the porch light. "Hi Little John."

I heard a grunt from behind me.

"Well, nothin,'" I said, trying to peek around Justine and Robyn.

"Come in and tell me," gushed Justine. "Don't stand on the porch."

"We brought Mountain Dew!" I heard the ever-familiar voice of dear Kiljoy calling. Someday, we will teach the boy some tact. "Bottles even!"

"Well, maybe we can play spin-the-bottle later," Justine chirped. Oh, that girl killed me.

Robyn reluctantly held the door open as we six young studs paraded in. Justine was our majorette, leading us to the glorious basement.

"We were just watching 'Breakfast at Tiffany's.'"

"I hope we're not interrupting," I said, always the gentleman.

"No! We've watched it a thousand times!"

Our procession ended in a theatre of overstuffed couches and beanbags horseshoed around the TV. A humidifier emitted a stream of steam. It was like we were inside the magic lamp and here was our treasure.

I heard a squeak over my shoulder.

"Chicks!"

10

A Dagger Is Only So Long

A busted beer bottle lying in the gutter. Rainwater and sewer sludge trickling along the curb and down into the rusted storm drain. A caravan of high school kids cruising the main strip. Hanging out the car windows. Yelling at other cars filled with giggly girls at the stoplight, revving the engine. Where's the party at? Then the light turns green and the tires squeal with adolescent criminality and innocence.

Have they been told of the Buddha? Chant the amidha and calm the citta. The path to salvation is now paved in concrete. At the crossing, you pay your toll, and they let you pass. No clarity, just the understanding that there is another toll ahead. And there is no refund.

What about Mohammed? Whom we never met. What does he have to offer and how much will it cost? Just your life. Give your life to Mohammed, and he shall bring you eternal sanctity. You must always give something, or else you cannot reap the benefits.

Promise of immortality. Promise of beauty. Promise of wealth. Promise of happiness. Promise of truth. It keeps spinning and we keep listening and we keep driving and we keep paying and we keep breeding, and we keep dying, but have you seen the globes? The spheres rotating infinitely.

We run as fast as we can, trying to catch up, but the race always ends, so we speed through life, chasing and anticipating every move, keeping faith in the fact that the faster we run, the better we are. Battles are fought, rationalities are killed. The race ends for some, while it's just beginning for others. The orbs never stop.

Few win the race. Jesus won. But then, Jesus didn't run.

Only broken glass lying on the pavement. Who threw it there? A rangy, broken man, stumbling down the street. He's not going anywhere, but he still knows that he needs to get somewhere. A few pennies here, a couple of quarters there, hey mister, do you have a dime to spare? I need a sandwich. My kids need to eat. My eyes are bleeding and my heart is beat. If I can just make it through today, tomorrow will be better.

Abraxas told me to join the team. One is all and all is one. One for one for none. I could be you and you could be me. I am earth and you are land. I came out screaming at birth, and I died, chasing the F-man.

11

DON'T CALL ME BOBBY

THE CALM A HUNTER FEELS WHEN HE HAS HIS PREY LINED UP IN THE CROSSHAIRS.

September 3, 1994

This is what Dr. Carter felt like when he opened Tutankhamun's tomb. A loss of consciousness, transcendence to another plane of reality. Euphoria. The treasures of a king.

There were others in Robyn's basement den. I only saw Melissa. She was scowling, but her babydoll eyes were only meant for me. Pleasantries were being exchanged with the other girls, and I believe I gave some of my own, but my thoughts were faithful to only one. The gorgeous petite girl, sitting on the couch, her arms crossed across her chest, her eyes shielded by a baseball cap. Tigers. But gazing out from the shadow of the bill, two gleams of light shone on me. Beckoning, daring me to advance. The challenge was made, the gloves were thrown down, and I was ready to draw my pistol. It's high noon. Time to be on your toes. Kill or be killed. The fastest draw wins the damsel.

Nothing ever felt so natural.

There was a space on the couch next to Melissa. I moseyed my way toward her. Spewing words at whoever was in my path, but alas, I was too slow. Mike had slithered his way next to her. I wheeled in the middle of the room. I must mark my territory somewhere. All seats were full. Cody was standing in the doorway, leaning against the frame. There's my base. My operational command center. Rendezvous point. Regroup and attack again.

Mike was blathering to Melissa, about biology, I believe. She feigned interest, those eyes kept flashing in my direction. Oh darling, soon. Soon I shall slay the dragon, and I will take you in my arms.

"So, how's it going?" I leaned my back against the wall next to Cody. His long sandy bangs dangled over his eyes and the locks in back touched his shoulders.

"All right," he mumbled.

"We're actually hanging out with girls, dude."

"Yeah, awesome."

"You gonna try to hook up?"

He just glanced at me. That was a pretty stupid thing to say. I better cool down. Cody's got it right. Chill, as if we have better things to do. Justine bopped over to us. She was a marshmallowy sparkplug.

"Did you hear what Trevor Klink did in gym today?" she asked, with a mouthful of smile.

"Yeah, I was there," I said. Goddamn Klink. The running back. Always scoring the touchdown, usually with his pants down.

"I can't believe he jumped in the swimming pool," gushed Justine.

"Yeah, out of control," mumbled Cody, slumping even further against the doorframe. I had to smirk at his refusal to embrace conformist culture. You create culture, you don't follow it.

"I hear he got suspended," Justine said, still all smiles.

"No, he just has to do catwalks for the next three gym classes," I said. I eyeballed Melissa again. She caught me in the act. Excellent. Good Lord she was so beautiful. She was wearing an over-sized, gray Western U sweatshirt, tight Levi's. Casual, yet classy. My girl.

Then Mike stood up. His fatal mistake. Or maybe he was just warming her up for me. I slipped away from the doorway, leaving Justine to blabber at Cody. No hesitation this time. I made a beeline for the couch.

"Is it all right if I share the couch with you?"

This was it. No turning back. It's crunch time. Eight ball, corner pocket. God, she's beautiful. Her lips a strawberry. Her nose a... grape.

"I guess so," she said. So cool. I felt a drawbridge reeling in. The bolt locked. But I had a key. I slumped my ass down next to hers, testing to see how much thigh contact she would allow. It wasn't much as she scooched away from me.

"I hope you don't mind us dropping by," I said. My shoulder was touching hers. I could feel the warmth and the energy emanating from her within. Stay cool, boy.

"No." The tone of her voice said otherwise, but it was just part of the game. They were having a better time without us. I know how it goes. Before we arrived, all they did was talk about us.

From across the room, Little John, who was sitting low in a beanbag chair like a pimply Buddha in blue jeans, gave me a thumbs up.

"We were just cruising around, y'know," I said. Dramatic pause. "I got a car today."

"Are you sixteen?" she asked, her voice, like Mariah, her glance, quizzical. She wanted to know more about me. She was new this year. Moved from Colorado. She was already star of the girls cross country team and had slid right in with the cool girls. But she didn't know yet about us boys. I was ready to tell her. Though more than likely, she already knew. Everybody knows who I am.

"Actually I just turned seventeen. Last week."

"You're a year older?" she asked. She wasn't going to make this easy. It was time to 'fess up. Yes, your honor, I shot down those schoolchildren and raped the nun, but I'm better now. God, she smelled good. The tender scent of her shampoo. Clean. So pure.

"Well... yeah."

"Were you held back a year?" Ouch. I felt my cheeks heat up. This was not going to be easy.

"Um... yeah." What could I say? "I had this ear thing when I was a kid."

"You smell like smoke," she groused. Her nose crinkled but her eyes still held the beacon. This was one hell of a hole to fill up.

"Yeah, er, yeah. We smoked some cigars before we came over here," I said. "In my car."

Play the bad boy. Keep her intrigued. "Celebration, and all," I added.

"Cigars are disgusting," she said, and looked away. She couldn't look me in the eye. Her bottom lip stuck out slightly, pouting. Oh, you're breaking my heart! Those angelic blue eyes, only, if just once, they would lay their glory in mine.

"Yeah, but they make us look cool," I said coyly, with a devilish grin.

What was that? I think she giggled. Bullseye.

"I mean, you know, it was a special occasion. We never gotta ride a bike again. We've got wheels. We have motor vehicle transportation. We are not mice. We are men."

I shook my fist.

She covered her lovely mouth with her delicate hand to hide her laughter. Shakespeare, eat your heart out. Robert Longley is on center stage.

"You're funny."

"Funny like a clown, or funny like Screech?" I asked. "I'd much rather you said Zack Morris."

"You wish," she giggled.

I was on a roll. She rolled her eyes, but they landed on mine. And we locked. Ode to Joy. She quickly tore her gaze away, and it was her turn to blush. I felt her body relax, and she nestled into my shoulder, just slightly.

"That was a nice catch you had in the game," she said. Was that a touch of reverence I heard in her voice?

"Were you at the game?" I asked, nonchalantly. I knew full well she was at the game. I could tell you her seat number. "Thanks, it was pretty lucky."

Then, like it was meant to be, she squeezed my bicep.

"You were the hero of the day."

A sledgehammer couldn't break the boner that popped into my pocket.

"I mean, it was nothing. I think I had my eyes closed, you know? It happened so fast I didn't have time to think. Keith was the one that threw the ball," I said, then I raised my voice in mock bravado. "We are a well-oiled machine, assembled of many separate parts, and I am just one of those many parts, churning to achieve team victory."

Oh, dear Melissa. How your laughter tickles my ears.

"You're too funny."

"Now you think I'm a clown," I said. I crossed my eyes. Melissa was but a beautiful blur over the tip of my nose. Juvenile, but effective. "There is so much more to me than a sick sense of humor."

Now it was my turn to act defiant. Appease me, baby. Let me talk about myself some more.

"Oh really, and what is there?"

"I'm not going to tell you. You gotta find out for yourself."

"It sounds like you are coming on to me."

Whoa! She broke the rules. This is no longer a game. Precedence must be set.

"You caught me. I suppose I am. Is that all right with you?"

I dropped my voice low, vulnerable. I laid my eyes heavy into hers, searching. I didn't know the words that were coming out of my mouth. My brain was a blank void and the words were being cast out by a ghostly typewriter. This conversation got way serious fast. We weren't fucking around anymore.

"No. It's not all right." Her stare could melt steel. It melted my heart.

"What if I ask you out?" I was whispering now. I could smell the cigar on my breath. Shit. Her face was just inches from mine. She didn't flinch.

"What if you were?"

Love. God, I'm in love.

"Would you say yes?"

"Maybe."

"Hey you two! You look awfully cozy there!" I jerked out of my Lemuria. Justine was in my face. Grinning, her jackal eyes gleaming. Both Melissa and I retracted back into our shells. But her shoulder still leaned into mine. Her thigh touched mine. We were one.

My job is done here. Time to bounce.

"Hey, you guys ready to roll?" I called out to the troops. Round 'em up. The herd has been corralled and the horses have been fed.

"We just got here," Kiljoy protested.

"Yeah, well we've got people to do and things to see. The party boat is pulling outta the harbor."

I reluctantly rose from my throne and faced my fair maiden.

"I'll call you," I said. I looked into those beautiful blue eyes. Lord, how could I ever look away. "G'night."

"Goodnight." The words barely escaped her lips. Touchdown.

I turned my back and triumphantly strode from the room, my soldiers following in rank file. Glory, glory, hallelujah. Joshua fought the battle of Jericho. The saints go marching on. Who stands? I stand. Who is much more the man? I'm much more the plan. I'm the F-man. The F-man Himself.

12

BITS AND PIECES

November 7, 1994

The swirl cone is the punt returner of the ice cream world. You get the best of both worlds. In the swirl cone, you get vanilla and chocolate. As a punt returner, you get to catch the ball and run with a head full of steam in the open field. The swirl cone was Robert's favorite ice cream treat. Punt returner was his favorite position on the football team.

Considering Coach Martin never wanted to pass it was the only time Robert got to touch the ball during a football game and in return show his open field moves.

Today, Robert was going to show Melissa his moves with the swirl cone.

Or something like that.

Robert had taken Melissa to Mickey D's for their first date. Their first alone time together. They had hung out in a group. They had gone with all their friends to the movie theater to watch "Pulp Fiction" twice. Robert loved Jules Winnfield. Melissa thought the movie was too long. Robert held her hand during the heroin scene. Mike was angry that John Travolta died.

His friends weren't here today. Football season was over. It was the first day Robert didn't have to go to practice after school. At the end-of-year banquet, Coach Martin had given every player that didn't receive an award, like MVP, which was given to that buttwipe Klink, a McDonald's gift certificate.

Robert asked Melissa if she wanted to get an ice cream cone after school. She said, "Yes."

Inside the restaurant, an afternoon get-together of retirees had taken up the center tables and were making a big stink about crop prices. Robert suggested they take their cones outside for peace and quiet.

Even though the November chill had set in, Melissa, who had also gotten a swirl cone, said, "Yes."

The outside of McDonald's was still decorated in plastic Halloween stringers you could buy at the dollar store. Pumpkins and witches. The brown brick building was located on the edge of downtown Crawford Falls, along the main four-lane road, at the intersection with the stoplight. Robert's house was somewhere across the street. He could walk home, but he drove his Civic.

Robert and Melissa sat down on the curb in front of McDonald's and ate their ice cream cones. Melissa took dainty little licks like a kitten lapping up milk. Robert wrapped his tongue around the bottom of the ice cream, swirling the vanilla and chocolate together.

Robert wore his red letterman jacket. Melissa wore an overstuffed CF Tigers sweatshirt and tight, acid-washed jeans. Her hair was pulled back in barrettes at the sides, revealing her ears, pink from the chill air, each with a simple gold stud earring. A silver cross necklace hung over her chest.

With one hand Melissa ate her ice cream. Her other hand was planted on the concrete curb. Robert placed his hand over hers. She didn't pull away.

Her hand was chilled to the bone. Her long, slim fingers fit inside Robert's thick, meaty fingers. Like one. The warmth of love rushed through Robert and enveloped his chest.

"Melissa," he said. "Um... will you be my girlfriend?"

Melissa said, "Yes."

Robert, who had wolfed down his ice cream cone, took off his letterman jacket and draped it over Melissa's shoulders. He pulled her close and nestled his nose in her blonde hair. It smelled of lavender. Lovely, lovely lavender.

13

THIS ONE'S FOR YOU

Love, love. What is love? Love is snuggling in front of the TV watching Mel Brooks movies. Even though Mel Brooks makes you laugh as hard as your grandfather's archaic jokes. Love is lying on the sixth green at night wrapped wound warmly in a wool blanket, gazing into the full moonlit spring sky. Whispering of dreams and fantasies and sweet sweet love.

The grass underneath you is damp, but you don't care. There's not a cloud in the sky, not a fear in your being. "I want to touch the stars," she says. She beams. Her eyes shimmer with heavenly bliss and her gold-spun hair tickles your cheek. You brush lips across her forehead. Her touch, her skin, her sensation, her temptation, her beauty her breath her being.

"There is no reason to visit the stars." Hush. Everything is going to be all right. A smile. A question. A lovely smile. Lovely lips. "Take comfort in knowing that they are protecting you." Because they are. And you are. Take comfort. Everything is going to be all right. I will protect you. I'm your star. I'm your rock star. What more can you ask for?

A castle in the clouds. To dance on the moon. A ring on the finger, a bundle in the safe, and family coming soon. To appease the father and suffer with the mother. Love the children and weep with my brothers. But the love shines through.

Can my hands go here? Can I put them here? How about there? Can I put my hands anywhere? You can put your lips here if you want. I can give you anything you want. I will give you everything you want. You want the stars? Baby, you got the stars. They call me the little prince. I'll give you anything you want. I'll give you a kiss.

Then the moon air lunar breaks. Her lips seal. Locked. Broken. Chaste. What is a boy to do? The breadbasket has been barred. Venus has come to collect her karma. What do you do boy? You have already eaten the apple. Nothing to do but laugh. Shake your head.

The stars are still shining down upon you. Tell her that. The stars will always be there to protect you. Twinkle, twinkle, little star. How I wonder what you are. Wrap her in your arms. Tell her everything is going to be all right. It's all inside of you and it is all outside of us.

And the stars surround us. The heavens still protect us. The sun still shines down upon us. And you still hold the hand of sweet Beatrice. A servant in a needy land. The treasure of the greedy man. I'm much more the plan. At battle I stand. All hail the F-man. The righteous man. The F-plan. Much more the man. The F-man Himself.

14

PROM 1995

April 29, 1995

The dance hall was filled with magic. Powder blue and white curtains and streamers were draped across the stage where the DJ booth towered like a pulpit that beamed shimmers of light and music. The spacious conference hall was dim, and spotlights rotated across the floor, splashing light on canoodling couples and groups of decked out teenagers huddled together in spastic gyration.

The energy of life was vibrant within the confines of the Four Seasons convention hall.

Melissa was in the bathroom washing her hands. Other girls were waiting their turn outside the toilet stall or preening their wavy coifs sticky with hairspray. Melissa let her natural blonde curls dangle with buoyancy. She was wearing a powder blue dress to match the prom theme. The shoulders of the dress were ruffled, the neckline cut off right there, just below her neck.

She and her mother spent two weekends searching for the dress. Driving to Sioux City and Omaha respectively, searching through the racks of each dress shop like explorers pulling back the jungle foliage. Her mother left no rack untouched. She spared no expense.

Melissa sighed.

She was here with Robert, of course. He never officially asked her to prom. It's not like she had wanted a proposal or anything, but it would have been nice if he had put some thought or care into it. Just one day they were in his basement watching MTV and out of the blue he said, "I guess I better get a tux."

That was it. They were going to prom together. Not only did Melissa spend weeks picking out the right dress she also picked out Robert's tuxedo to make sure it matched and to stop him from getting that stupid *Dumb and Dumber* tuxedo all the idiots were wearing. She took Robert to the flower shop to select the white corsage pinned to her chest.

Melissa did all the work, and still Robert found a way to put a damper on her magical night.

He refused to stand for professional photographs in front of the angelic background set up at the entrance of the dance hall. He said it was a waste of money. A shill trying to make a buck off the inherent conformist nature of teenagers, or something like that, is what Robert said.

Melissa had to agree or else devolve into a bitter argument that would leave her in tears and smeared mascara. Not tonight. They took pictures beforehand at her parents' house. That would have to suffice.

Justine and Rachel were in the bathroom with her sharing the mirror, teasing their hair, and dabbing their lips with gloss. Justine wore a bedazzled mauve dress that showed off her ample bosom. Her cheeks were dappled with glitter. It was cute.

"Did you see Carolyn Larson's dress?" asked Justine in a snide tone. "Gross."

"It's like it came from Goodwill," snickered Rachel, who towered over Melissa and Justine, wearing a plain white dress that frilled at the collar, her long brown hair wavy like Daisy Duke.

"I don't know," murmured Melissa. "It's unique."

"Yeah, well," started Rachel, nodding quickly in agreement. "She has her own style."

"She's a lesbian!" guffawed Justine. The other two girls stifled their laughter as they exited the bathroom.

The dance floor heaved with vibrating teenagers as the DJ bumped that "Hip Hop Hooray" song. Melissa preferred Faith Hill.

"Where are those morons?" Justine shouted over the music.

By "those morons," she was referring to their dates—Robert, Little John, and Cody. Justine was going out with Little John now. Melissa and Robert had convinced Cody to begrudgingly ask Rachel out to prom so they could all team up. The six of them had gone out to dinner at the fancy Italian place where Melissa ordered the salad. She told Robert to get the fettuccine with Alfredo sauce so he didn't splatter marinara all over his shirt.

Then Robert drove her and Cody and Rachel to the dance in his dad's Lincoln while Little John and Justine followed in John's station wagon. The disagreement over the photos happened as soon as they arrived at the Four Seasons, and it still had Melissa agitated. At least they didn't have to stand in line forever, so maybe it wasn't so bad.

The DJ started playing that Boyz II Men song she liked, and her nerves were soothed, at least until she found Robert. Somehow, he had found a pair of red, oversized sunglasses that had plastic frames shaped like stars. He was standing on a chair slow dancing by himself pretending to sing into a rolled-up handbill.

Melissa had helped design those handbills.

"Robert!" she said in her loudest voice. Startled, Robert spotted her and gave her a big ol' grin. His hair, which had been slicked back with wax, was tussled, greasy red strands hanging out to the side. He hopped down from the chair, stumbled, and grabbed her hand. His hand was sweaty.

"Let's dance!" he yelled. Melissa took off his sunglasses, put them on the table, and patted down his hair. Then she allowed him to drag her out to the dance floor. Robert certainly was debonair in his tuxedo.

The party lights dimmed and sprayed the crowd with yellow LED pellets. The song was "Wonderful Tonight" by Clapton. Robert squeezed Melissa by the waist, and they gently rocked back and forth, Melissa's arms draped over his shoulders.

"This is it," murmured Robert. "This is everything."

Melissa simpered at Robert, locking her eyes on his. The top of her head reached Robert's chin. Robert could smell her lavender shampoo. He lifted her chin and leaned in, giving Melissa a peck on the lips. Melissa's smile grew, then she looked away, her eyes downcast.

"What's wrong?" asked Robert.

"I'm sorry," she said, looking at Robert again. "I'm sorry I was upset."

"No, don't be," said Robert. "I'm sorry. It's no big deal."

"I just want it to be a special night," said Melissa, with a slight whimper. Her face was like a baby deer in the moonlight.

"Me too," said Robert, his reassuring smile showing the gap between his front teeth. Melissa gave a broader smile. Her dry eyes focused on Robert's throat.

"Robert," she said with a gulp. "I think... I think I love you."

Robert's eyes shined.

"I love you, too," he gushed. His heart was warm. It could stay like this forever.

"Hey," he added, lowering his head in close to hers. "Brett Cardell said they're gonna have a party later... out off Union Road."

Melissa was silent, her thin lips agape.

"But..." she started. "What about After Prom?"

"What about it?"

"Robert, I'm on the committee."

"So, it's not like they need you," said Robert, a pleading in his voice.

"Robert," said Melissa, sternly. "It's my responsibility."

"Yeah," said Robert meekly. "Yeah, of course. We'll go to After Prom."

Melissa gave Robert a cold look.

"Good," she said.

"It'll be fun," said Robert, his broad smile returned. "Little J and Keith'll be there."

The duo swayed to the music, taking in the lyrics, hoping the lights would bring their spirits back up. They didn't.

"Um, I heard something," said Robert, haltingly. "But it's really stupid."

"What is it?" asked Melissa quietly.

"It's nothing," said Robert. "Really, it's nothing. Never mind."

"Nothing?"

"Well, it's about you...," said Robert.

"About me?"

"It was just something, they were saying earlier..."

"Who?" asked Melissa.

"Nobody," said Robert. "It's nothing."

"If it was about me, then it wasn't nothing," said Melissa.

"Well..." Robert stuttered.

"Robert," said Melissa. "What is it?"

The song ended. Robert and Melissa stood in the middle of the dance floor. The other couples had dispersed to the edges hall. Robert and Melissa stood there like statues under a waterfall of disco light.

"Well, I heard that some of the girls from the cross country team said...," mumbled Robert. "I know it's not true. It's so stupid. But I thought you should know. They said... They said, like, at your old school, in Colorado, that like, you used to, like, give lots of BJs."

The silence was a knife.

"BJs?" said Melissa.

"I know it's not true," said Robert, as the dance music started up again and kids filtered back on to the dance floor. "I just..."

Melissa had turned. She ran off the dance floor, holding her skirt bunched up at her knees. Robert hurried after her into the recesses of teenage heaven. He lost her as she disappeared into the girl's bathroom.

***

In the bathroom, Melissa was once again drying tears from her eyes. She sucked in the sobs. Justine and Rachel found her there. They formed a wall to hide Melissa from the looky-loos.

"He's such a jerk," cursed Justine, offering up a tissue to Melissa.

"Why would he say that?" choked Melissa.

"I'll murder those bitches," growled Rachel.

"Hey, listen," said Justine, soothingly. "You know Kyle Sommers?"

"Yeah," said Melissa.

Kyle Sommers was a senior. He was captain of the boys cross country team. All-state. Melissa watched him from afar during practice. All the girls did. He was tall, lean, with wavy brown hair and a million-watt smile. Melissa tried to catch glimpses of him at church, which was difficult because his family always sat up in the balcony.

Rumor had it Kyle earned a scholarship to Cornell—the one in New York.

"I heard he likes you," whispered Justine with a sly smile on her full, glossy lips.

"He does?" asked Melissa, dabbing tissue at her moist cheeks.

***

Robert stood outside the girls' bathroom, hands in the pockets of his tuxedo pants. The pockets felt like tent fabric. He watched the other teenagers dance. He looked at how happy they were.

Robert wanted to be happy.

15

BOY MUST BE BLIND

August 19, 1996

In 1492, Columbus sailed the ocean blue.
By 1495, Columbus had taken all the natives' lives
There are many facts folks say to you,
But if you listen closely,
There are many more truths.

***

Reverend Brewer was not good at respecting silences. He wanted to allow his passenger his space. Let him talk when he was well and ready. However, Reverend Brewer was well and ready to talk.

"Where are you coming from?" Reverend Brewer asked, scanning the highway rolling past.

"St. Louis," said Robert, tearing his eyes from the passenger window.

"What's going on there?"

"Nothin'."

"There's a lot going on in Saint Louie. I can't imagine you were doing just nothin' there."

Robert sighed.

"Hey look, I'm sorry if you don't want to talk about it," said Reverend Brewer. "I get curious. Snoopy really."

Reverend Brewer chuckled, his laugh deep and soulful.

"No, I'm sorry," said Robert. "It's just been a tough few days. It's hard to talk about."

"I get it," said Reverend Brewer. "I help out a lot of kids in similar situations. There are some things in life that are too painful for words."

Reverend Brewer looked over at Robert. Robert's skin was pale. His cheeks were drawn back. He still had a healthy glow in his eyes and confidence in his manner. Reverend Brewer dealt with a lot of runaways. Kids who were fed needles of drugs by their mothers. Teenage girls that had been prostituted out by their uncles. Those kids had a hollowness in their eyes that could never be filled.

This boy, Robert. He was strung out, to be sure, but his soul wasn't out of reach. In Reverend Brewer's honest opinion, Robert was a white boy from the suburbs who stumbled down the wrong alley and needed someone to lead him out.

"Do you have family in Crawford Falls?" asked Reverend Brewer. His tongue had a mind of its own.

Reverend Brewer knew of Crawford Falls. It was a small university town. He watched the Cougars basketball team during March Madness. It was also a sundown town where the Blacks somehow had difficulty finding jobs above menial labor.

It was these sorts of towns that Reverend Brewer was drawn to. He wanted to enlighten the mainstream. He also enjoyed giving a little scare to Midwest housewives.

"Yeah," said Robert. "My folks're there."

"Mom and Dad?" asked Reverend Brewer. "They still together?"

"Mm hm."

Reverend Brewer took that as a "yes."

"Your parents are probably wondering where you are," said Reverend Brewer.

"They know where I am," said Robert. "They don't care."

Reverend Brewer pondered this response. He knew he was treading in delicate waters. Of course Robert's parents cared where he was. That's what parents do. Even the junkie moms who lose their babies to foster care still care where their children are sleeping.

Still, it amazed Reverend Brewer how big of a divide the kids perceived in such situations. The parents saw a crack in the sidewalk. Kids saw the Grand Canyon.

"You know, I have four kids of my own," said Reverend Brewer. "I can hardly keep track of where they are."

The newscaster on the radio was reporting on an earthquake in Alaska. Reverend Brewer and Robert listened to the report intently. Earthquakes in America were an oddity. Finally, Robert spoke, almost elegantly. He became animated for the first time since Reverend Brewer had picked him up.

"Did you know that from 1870 to 1970 there was an average of like two to six earthquakes per decade, and from 1970 to 1990, that went way up to like 50 earthquakes per decade?" asked Robert. "And this decade alone there've already been 200 earthquakes?"

"Two hundred and one, now," the reverend added.

"And there's nothing we can do about it," continued Robert. "We've tried so hard to protect ourselves from destruction. Star Wars defense program, bomb shelters, F-16 stealth bombers, SCUD missiles, chemical warfare, it's all worthless. Mother Nature is going to get us in the end."

"Or God," said the reverend, raising his eyebrows at the boy. Robert retreated to the window.

"That's my job, you know," the reverend continued. "I preach the word of God."

Robert grunted in acknowledgement.

"Do you attend church?"

"Not since confirmation."

"Do you believe in God?"

Robert sighed. "I believe in something."

"What's that?"

"Well...," Robert began, and then gazed out the window. He ran his tongue around his lips. He gave a quick glance to Reverend Brewer then looked straight out the windshield.

"The Indians believed in one holy spirit that resided in everything, every tree, flower, rock, was embodied by the Great Spirit," Robert said, almost recited. "Pretty much the same as the Shinto religion in Japan, only with individual kami, or gods, that lived inside their own piece of nature. The natives, the Indians, Americans, lived their lives, devoting every action to their Great Spirit. Put back into the earth what they take out. Leave no trace, you know. They didn't cheat, steal, or lie. They were trustworthy, loyal, helpful, friendly, courteous, kind, obedient, cheerful, thrifty, brave, clean, and reverent. Followed the Golden Rule to the tooth. And one day, they get word that the white man's preacher is coming, a missionary, to talk with them about God. So they all dress up wearing, you know, their version of their Sunday's best, headbands and beads and whatnot, to welcome their guest. And this white man comes and tells them that they are doing it wrong. They are worshipping the wrong God. He tells them that... that they're nothing but pagan savages. He must convert them and correct the errors of their ways. And this he does... with force. Those who didn't convert to Christianity and swear against their so-called pagan gods were cast out, or worse. Which God is just? How do we get to decide which God is better than someone else's? So, I mean, tell me revered, who's God do you worship?"

It was Reverend Brewer's turn for silence.

"I'm sorry, I don't mean disrespect," mumbled Robert. "I just get worked up over the subject. I believe in God, the problem is that church always puts me to sleep. Especially on a Sunday morning."

The reverend chuckled from his belly.

"I understand, son. I won't ask you again."

Robert laughed also and leaned his head back into the headrest. Dark green rows of corn dominoed along the road. The sun was riding low in the sky, painting the few wispy Cirrus clouds pink and orange. The newscaster on the radio was now reading the weather, clear and sunny for the rest of the week.

Robert closed his eyes, but he knew he wouldn't sleep. He just felt the rolling hum of the highway, churning underneath the wheels of the car.

"I guess, I feel that the only reason I am here is because someone is allowing me to."

16

SILENCE DOGOOD BITES THE BIG ONE

June 21, 1995

Robert held the steering wheel at the bottom leading his Honda Civic down a gravel country road with his left thumb and forefinger. With his right hand he lit his Swisher Sweet cigar. His junior year of high school was well in the rear-view mirror.

Robert was wearing his track shirt and shorts. The season had gone well enough. He made it to state as an alternate for the sprint medley relay. There he cheered on Melissa as she brought home the gold as anchor of the girls' four-by-eight team. They were royalty at the end-of-year banquet.

Now all that was in Robert's headlights were summer nights and make-out sessions. At least until football camp next month.

"It's good to be a rock star," Robert said, his eyes gleaming as he glanced sideways at Cody who was riding shotgun. The glowing red ember at the end of Robert's stogie cyphered smoke into his face. Robert rolled down the window and puffed out a cloud.

"I don't know if being a rock star is all it's cracked up to be," Cody answered, hands tucked under the armpits of his gray Lemonheads T-shirt. Nobody else was in the car this time.

"What are you talking about?" laughed Robert. "What else is there? Either you're somebody or you're nobody. Anyone can be a nobody. Anyone can crawl into their sheltered home, draw the curtains, pretend that the rest of the world doesn't exist. But the rock star is the one who really lives."

"Lives for what?" asked Cody. "You're just living for everybody else. Life has no meaning, just pleasing someone else. Your fans, your manager, your agent, your producer, everyone but yourself. People who will turn on you in an instant."

"Fuck 'em!" laughed Robert.

"I'd rather set up shop in suburbia," continued Cody. "Nothing wrong with that. Have a family, teach English, write a book or two. Have a little peace and quiet. That's what life is about... personal satisfaction... not letting anybody else decide how you get to live your life. That's freedom, man."

Cody turned his face away from the pungent smoke creeping under his nostrils. He rolled down the window and the screaming summer wind tore into his face.

"Yeah, I mean, that's my back-up plan. If I can't be a rock star, I'm going to be a writer, too," hollered Robert. "Buy a nice cottage in the woods and make sweet, sweet love to Melissa every night. Write the great American novel. Go climb Mount Kilimanjaro, just like Hemingway. But to play music, in front of a screaming crowd! That's fuckin' life. Remember when we played the variety show? Everyone screaming our names? We hadn't even started yet! We could make it big, man. All it takes is the dedication and the fuckin' drive."

"I guess I just don't have it," said Cody. His shaggy, sandy-blonde bangs whipped at his pimply face. The pitch-black night sang into his ears. The steamy wind caressed his cheeks.

It was a balmy, muggy summer night, but then they all were. Being the only two of their friends without a summer job, Robert and Cody, and of course Melissa, were usually the only ones out late. Cody was growing weary of being the third leg.

Reading Cody's mind, Robert spoke up.

"You know what you need?" said Robert. His voice grated in Cody's ear. "You need a girlfriend. I could hook you up with one of Melissa's friends. I think Carolyn kind of likes you. And she's cute enough."

"Thanks, but no thanks," said Cody. Carolyn was cute, but as thick as plywood.

"I really think Melissa's the one," continued Robert, ignoring his friend's ever-increasing sourness. "She's the reason I get up in the morning. She's the reason I can't sleep at night. She's the only reason I went to school last semester. I mean, we'll just like talk on the phone, and I'll hold the phone to my ear just listening to her breathe for hours."

They were driving through town now. They cruised by box houses, bathed in orange light from the streetlamps.

"Yeah?" Cody feigned interest.

"Yeah, dude," said Robert, taking a long drag on his cigar. "Saturday's Melissa's birthday. I'm gonna take her to the Chester. I'm going to try to get laid."

He giggled with anticipation.

"Great," said Cody, swiping a stray, flapping strand of hair from his face.

Silence once again filled the cabin of the Honda Civic except for the ever-familiar chuckle of the engine and the air sweeping through the cabin.

"Brett Cardell and Chad Hicks asked me to play drums for them," said Robert. He was somber now.

"Yeah?"

"Yeah, we're going to practice next week," Robert said, glancing over at his friend. "You should come over. You can show 'em a thing or two."

"Sure, why don't you give me a call."

Robert pulled into Cody's driveway. The enormous gray home towered in the night.

"See you in the morning," said Robert.

"Yeah, going to breakfast tomorrow?"

"Every Tuesday and Thursday."

"All right, see ya."

"Yeah, later."

The door slammed. Robert backed out of the driveway his hand resting on the bottom of the steering wheel. He tossed the butt of the Swisher Sweet out of the window. He headed home to call Melissa.

17

[ADD SOMETHING ELSE]

White granite shards, glinting and sparkling from the morning sunlight, are surrounded by swirling gravel and dust cajoled by whirring automobiles. Destinations. Desperately trying to break the sound barrier. Across the Missouri Plain, the world is revolving, the sun brings on the new day. Mother sun. Bringing life, setting life in motion. A man stands on the side of the road. Trying his best to keep his ground, trying not to be thrown off the rolling sphere. Life whirs by, yet he stands still. Lost in time. Hesitant to blast out the barrel. Not ready to pull the trigger. As soon as the bullet leaves the chamber its course is set. Whether or not it hits its target it is all over. The screeching, screaming, whirring, whizzing, wild rush comes to a stop. What's a man got? Just a man. Standing on the road. Trying to stop. But the spheres keep spinning. The spheres never stop.

18

(SOMETHING YOU FORGOT)

June 24, 1995

S oul Coughing blared through Robert's Kenwood car speakers with three-cube subwoofers vibrating on the back dash. With every pound of bass the aluminum Honda rattled with weariness. The plastic wrap of the CD lay in his lap. He had ripped it open as soon as Melissa set it in his hands. Now he bobbed his head to the beat.

Robert glanced over at Melissa. Her eyes were red and puffy. She had bawled after she had opened her birthday gifts. Robert borrowed money from his pops and had bought a dozen red roses—six white ones to represent Melissa and six red roses to symbolize him. He also gave her a book of poetry. His poetry.

Melissa, dear Melissa
Your hair is as blue as the moon
Your skin as soft as silk
Your lips as sweet as wine
And your breast as white as milk.

That sort of bullshit. It broke her up. He gave it to her right after dinner. Robert had taken her to Garibaldi's for their one-year anniversary. She had the salad. Robert had the pasta Alfredo.

"I'm gonna stop for gas," said Robert, gazing at his girl. Melissa was wearing a skimpy, flowered sundress. The white bra-strap tangled with the string shoulder straps, and it had been driving Robert crazy all night. He was now staring down at her bronzed cleavage.

"You just passed the Quik-Mart," Melissa said, her tanned, toned arm pointing to the gas station as Robert drove right past it.

"Oh, whoops," he said. He took a sharp left and cruised next to a gas pump. "You need anything?"

"Can you get me some gum?"

"Yeah, I'll be right back."

Robert climbed out of the driver's seat. He leaned against his newly waxed car with his arms folded as the gallons and price gauges whizzed higher. The pump chunked abruptly for Robert as he released the trigger, just before the pump hit five dollars.

He ambled into the gas station. Robert was wearing his favorite black linen slacks and his suede black and white Hush Puppies. His overstuffed olive polo shirt hid his stringy body.

Inside, Robert dropped a pack of spearmint gum on the counter.

"Anything else?" the college-aged clerk asked.

"Yeah, can I get a pack of Marlboro Lights?" Robert didn't make eye contact.

"Do you have any ID?"

Robert slid his wallet out of his back pocket and rummaged through his various cards. He paused briefly to finger a condom.

"Shit," He muttered. "I must have left it at home."

The clerk looked Robert over quizzically.

"Just don't let it happen again," he said, and handed Robert the pack of smokes. "Your total is nine-nineteen."

"Thanks," Robert said after receiving his change.

Robert rubbed his silky goatee as he walked back to his car. The facial hair and off-kilter wardrobe allowed Robert to pass as a university student every time. He was almost eighteen anyway. He settled himself behind the steering wheel and strapped his seat belt.

"Thank you," said Melissa, smiling meekly as Robert handed her the gum.

Robert gazed into her eyes and a shudder ran from his neck to his groin. Her eyes were scorched red, but she had composed herself elegantly after her emotional breakdown.

"Where are we going?" she asked.

"The Chester," Robert answered. He cranked the ignition. The music resumed blaring through the speakers, and he backed out of the Quik-Mart.

"Where?" asked Melissa, turning down the radio.

"The Chester. It's a surprise."

"Sounds interesting."

It was times like this that Robert truly detested his car. He longed to have Melissa snuggled against his shoulder her fingers caressing the side of his face as he cruised down the country lanes. Instead, she was staring distractedly out the window in the damned bucket seat. Robert reached over and laid his hand atop hers, which were cradled in her lap. She jumped, having her trance broken. Melissa realigned her blank gaze to face out the windshield, her elven body rigid.

"Have I told you how beautiful you are?" asked Robert, squeezing her hand.

"Only three times tonight," said Melissa, giving him a weak smile. The hum of the road and the loose gravel bouncing off the Honda's side panel encompassed the restricting interior of the car.

"You know, Brett Cardell's throwing a party next weekend. You wanna go?" asked Robert, throwing a sidelong look at his girlfriend.

"You want to go to that party? Everybody's just going to get drunk and high. Really, Robert, I don't see why you would want to hang out with those guys. They're so... sleazy," chastised Melissa, slipping her hand out from under Robert's. She crossed her arms, clinging her hands in tight.

"Cardell's a cool guy. You should hear him play guitar," said Robert, his voice becoming defensive. "Him, Hicks, and me are thinkin' about starting a band. We might jam together at the party, you know, like a show."

"What about Keith, Cody, and John?"

It was Robert's turn to get dour.

"They aren't serious about it," he groused. "I mean, we have fun and all, but the band is shitty. If I play drums with Cardell and Hicks, we might, I don't know, maybe record an album."

"But they're such jerks."

"Well, yeah, sometimes they get a little out of hand..."

"A little out of hand?" Melissa interrupted. "What about at Homecoming? They were so wasted, and then setting off the bottle rockets... someone could have been hurt..."

Robert was thinking as hard as he could. Why didn't Melissa understand how cool Cardell and Hicks were? Was it because they didn't play football? Robert was thinking about dropping off the team anyway. Coach Martin only ran run plays out of the I formation. Robert was tired of blocking all game.

On this night, all Robert could do was stare Melissa's fiery eyes blazing him down. He wanted to be sucking on those pouty, agitated lips so badly. He wanted her fingers running through his hair...

"...and then the dog chased after the cheerleaders..."

...his hands slowly stroking her back. Robert had been waiting for this night for ages. Sure, they had made out. As soon as they were alone, Robert couldn't help himself from groping for every last bit of love that Melissa would allow. She fended him off fairly well, even though she did let him cop a feel once. Other than that, their romantic life was vanilla. Tonight was Robert's night. No way would Melissa be able to resist his charms.

"...and then the sprinkler system went off and the whole ceremony was ruined."

"I thought it was pretty funny," said Robert with a smirk. Then he added, "Cardell is president of the Student Council at least."

"That's because his campaign fliers were pasted with pictures of... of... naked women," griped Melissa.

Robert chuckled. He still had two of the fliers hanging on his bedroom wall.

Melissa's tirade had brought some sparks into the car, and Robert couldn't wait to turn that anger into passion.

"So you know the story about the Chester family?" Robert asked as he turned off Union Road and onto a level B dirt road. His headlights pierced through the black summer night and bounced off the overgrowth lining the road.

"No," Melissa pouted.

"Well, in the seventies, the Chester family owned a farm out here that Mr. Chester inherited from his dad. In fact, it's just two miles down the road," said Robert as he turned on his high beams. "The Chester family was fairly wealthy. They had quite a bundle stashed away. There were two children, ages five and two, and it was a very happy, content family, y'know. Anyway, Mr. Chester had this cousin out in New York, the oddball of the family. He was a bum, or something. One day, this cousin in New York just flips. He steals this VW Bug and drives all the way to Iowa without stopping. He goes to the farm, and in the dead of night, shoots, and kills, every member of the Chester family. All while they were sleeping. Even the two little innocent kids. Then he gets in his Bug and drives all the way back to New York."

"What happened to him?" asked Melissa, her mouth agape.

"Well, they caught him. He's in jail. He's actually up for parole in a few years."

"What are we doing out here, then?" asked Melissa, her tone shrill.

"This is where we are going," said Robert. He pulled over onto the shoulder of the dusty road and shined his headlights on an iron archway large enough for a small tractor to fit through shrouded by dogwood and overgrown weeds. "The Chester Cemetery," read the rusted sign hanging from the arch.

"Cemetery?" asked Melissa.

"Yeah. The Chester. It's the family graveyard. The entire family is buried here," said Robert, putting the car in park.

"Really?"

"Yeah, come on. I'll show you," Robert said, leaping out of the car. He ran to the other side and opened the door for Melissa. She gingerly stepped out of the car the heals of her strappy shoes squishing into the soft earth.

"It's cold out," she said, shivering. The car headlights shone on the cemetery, and Melissa could see silhouettes of gravestones on the other side of the cemetery's barbed wire fence.

"Let me get something," said Robert, and he popped open his trunk. He pulled out a wool blanket, a bottle of Boone's wine, and two plastic cups.

"What's that?" Melissa asked.

"It's to celebrate your birthday," said Robert with a bright smile. "Sweet seventeen."

"You brought wine?" asked Melissa. She didn't look happy.

"Yeah, I thought we would have some fun," said Robert. His spirits started to drain.

"I don't drink, Robert."

"It's just wine."

"It's alcohol."

"Just this once. Come on. It's a special night."

"I can't believe this. First you bring me to a creepy cemetery, then you want me to drink booze?"

"I didn't think you would mind. I'm... I'm sorry. We can leave if you want."

"No, look, Robert," Melissa stammered.

"I'm sorry," said Robert. He took a few steps toward Melissa, fluttering his puppy dog eyes, his arms outstretched to embrace her. His long, swooping hair curled around his ears like ram horns.

"Robert," said Melissa, stepping away from him, her stringy arms huddling her scrawny body. "We need to talk."

"What?" said Robert, stopping dead in his tracks. "What about?"

"I think we should break up," Melissa blurted. She stared at the hallowed ground.

"Break up? Why?" Robert's jaw hung slack. His face drained.

"There's just no flame between us anymore."

"No flame? What?"

"It's like we are a candle that just slowly burned out," said Melissa, her blonde hair in wavy curls, dangling down over her forlorn face, her gaze never wavering from the ground.

Robert could only stare at her. His angel. His perfect, beautiful angel. And now she was flying away.

"What did I do? Please don't..."

Robert reached for her again. Melissa shuddered away. Robert shook his head and walked to hood of the car. He leaned over and placed his hand on the hood.

"There's this guy..." Melissa started.

"What?"

Robert wheeled to face her.

"This guy from my church, Kyle. He asked me out," said Melissa. She stole a glance up at Robert's horrified face. "I think I'm going to say yes."

"Kyle Sommers?" shrieked Robert, dumbfounded. "That asshole?"

"He's a nice guy," whimpered Melissa.

Robert's arms hung limp at his sides. The dogwood trees lining the cemetery rustled in the breeze.

"If that's what you want," he heard himself say.

"Yes. Yes, it is."

"I guess I should drive you home."

"I think so."

***

After Robert watched Melissa run up her front steps and slam the door to his heart forever he went back to the Chester Cemetery. There, he drank the bottle of wine to the last drop, smoked the entire pack of cigarettes, and he cried and cried and cried.

19

God Is Lying

October 12, 1995

G otta look cool, man. Just look cool. Get your hands out of your pockets, it looks like you're playing with yourself. Steady now, don't look like an ass. Christ, there's a lot of people out there. No faces, just heads. Looking.

Little John is at the mic now, hulking on the pep rally stage in his blazing football jersey. Big game tomorrow night. A bead of sweat dripped down my armpit. Shit, that was cold. Cardell's on my left, a huge, goofy grin is on his face. Stoned as fuck. His slick, black hair is pulled into a topknot, sticking straight up in the air. Looks cool as hell, just wearing cut-off fatigues and a Hawaiian shirt. I look like a dork in my khakis and polo shirt. Hicks is standing on the stage next to Cardell. Also looking cool as fuck, ripped biceps crossed in front of his massive chest squeezing at his white undershirt.

Keith is at my right. He has the same look on his face as Cardell, only without the bleary-eyed daze. He's got stars in his eyes. At least Mom didn't make me wear a tie like Keith.

I haven't even seen my parents yet. They better be here, somewhere up there in the stands. The stage was erected in the middle of the practice football field. I was standing on the stage in line with the other doofuses.

Mom and Dad wouldn't miss their son standing on the Homecoming court, possibly to be crowned king, would they? I got as good a shot as any of these jokers. Cody's standing next to Keith, squirming like a nightcrawler on a hook. Flinching in the spotlight when they called his name. Ya gotta grab the spotlight, man. You don't get too many chances in life. You have to take advantage of your moment in the sun.

Little John just got done exploding on stage. "Go Tigers!" The principal is talking now. Our princely pal.

Justine is seated in a folding chair in front of me, beaming. She smells damned good, like bubblegum. Melissa is up here on stage as well. Sitting in front of fucking Klink. She'll win for sure. Hottest girl in school. And once she was mine. There's that familiar ache, the one that I know so well.

That ball of yarn knitted inside my stomach.

Every time I see her, it rises in my chest, clutching at my heart like a squirrelly hamster. Smiling only makes it hurt worse. Look at her, her curly, blonde hair, dangling perfectly over her shoulder. Shining under the floodlights. Her soft face, oh, and those crystal eyes. If only I could melt into them one more time everything would make sense again.

Look at me. Look at me, Melissa. Please.

But here we are. The moment of reckoning. The crowd is cheering as the principal finishes his speech. He has an envelope in his hand. The crowd is so far away. I can't make out any faces. But I know they're looking. And those lights are so bright, hot.

"And the Homecoming King is..."

No lumps, no shakes, am I nervous at all.

"Robert Longley."

Ow, shit. Someone pinches my ass, hard. I step forward, squeezing between Justine's and Carrie's chairs.

"Excuse me," I mumble. What's going on? A crown is on my head. So much applause. Hollers and whistles and catcalls. My face burns up. The principal shakes my hand. Then he leaves me there, standing, smiling, no faces, not one face.

The bright emptiness is overwhelming.

"And the Homecoming Queen is..."

Dramatic pause as he unseals the envelope.

"Melissa Campbell."

Uproar. Clap, clap, I clap. She stands, an angel. She covers her mouth, eyes popping, and stands from her chair. She looks at me. She comes to me. She is next to me. I feel her heat, her excitement. A tiara is placed on her head, roses thrust into her arms. She locks eyes with me. So much love, so much joy. Yes, Lord. It is so right. I spread my arms, and she falls into my chest. I hold her. It's been so long since her warm body was cradled in my arms. She's crying, sobbing. I stroke her hair, as she shakes. Never let go. I'll never let go. My queen. My angel. My reason.

Then she releases from my grip. And she embraces the principal. And she hugs Justine. And she hugs Carrie, and Liz, and Keith. And Cardell swings her around. And I stare. Clap, clap, I clap. Alone once again. Alone, dying under the spotlight. Who's the king? Who's the rock star?

What more can you ask for.

***

I lay in peace upon my bed
I free my mind and gain control
No more worries to fill my head
Search for Jesus to save my soul.
Beat out the pleasure til it can take no more
Soothe the pain and remember the glow
The core is hot but the shell is sore
Cork up the hole and stop the flow.
The blood runs when he is put on the cross
He suffered and died to cleanse me of my sins
But I say to myself, it was no big loss
The sun still shines, and Jesus will rise again.

20

WHAT ARE YOU GOOD FOR?

November 25, 1995

This girl

has no clue

what my world is.

Darkness,

refracts.

Pain,

reflects.

And it all weighs down.

***

I strained my wrist, grunting, wedging the nut on my bass drum pedal tight. Satisfied with the snugness, I returned my drum key to the pocket of my Levi's. I happily pounded with my brand-new Gibraltar double-bass pedal. My left foot was still weak. Instead of a steady thump-thump, thump-thump, like a jack-hammer, I sounded more like a galloping horse, da-thum, da-thum, da-thump.

If Melissa could see me now.

I was set up in the garage. Sawdust covered the concrete floor, and a decon-structed Suzuki 250cc motorcycle languished in the corner. Hicks was smoking a cigarette, thumping out a blues minor sevenths progression. Cardell was still tuning his guitar. Damn guitarists. Cardell's a good one, though.

Cardell and I were in jazz band together, if you can believe it. Even though Cardell wasn't in orchestra they made an exception for him to join. He won the state solo contest for playing his guitar behind his head.

Then Cardell and Hicks and a couple of other Northies got caught sneaking up on the roof of the hardware store after midnight to smoke doobies. Cardell got kicked out of jazz band. He also got kicked off the student council, which he was kinda glad about.

Ever since Homecoming Cardell and Hicks had taken me under their wing. Cardell bartended at his uncle's place in Alton and we'd head over there after school. His uncle let us use the garage next to his bar for practice space. An electric space heater glowed orange next to Cardell's amplifier.

Cardell finally finished tuning and let out a mean riff that would have rivaled Stevie Ray. Only heavier and louder. And I've never seen anyone hammer the bass like Hicks. That fucker is all over that thing, slapping out notes that don't exist, riffs that make the fault lines tremble. I keep us grounded. With my new double-bass though, I can open an entire new dimension of sound.

This band kicks ass. We already have a gig lined up. We're opening at Ruby's for this metal showcase. The headliner, Wormhole, is one of the best live shows I have ever seen. They have a distorted, screeching, screaming, tormented, hellish sound that shivers up and down the double helix of my DNA. I've never seen the other headliner play, Violent Sunshine.

This will be my first real show. I mean, besides the time Cody, I, and the rest of the guys played the talent show last spring. Besides, we sucked. Cody broke a string in the middle of his solo and Keith made Alfalfa sound like Sinatra. Oh well, no one noticed. They all loved it, especially Melissa. Man, that was just six months ago.

I kinda lost touch with those guys. Keith is always out of town visiting his girlfriend. Little John's still dating Justine, so he's always on double dates with Melissa. I tried to get Cody to join our band, but he made an excuse for being busy. I haven't seen him outside of school in weeks.

We stopped going to breakfast on Tuesdays and Thursdays. We never said anything about it. One Tuesday we just didn't go, and that was it.

"What should we play first?" I hollered.

"We need to start this session with a little prayer," Cardell answered, plucking at an errant guitar string "And I think Mary Jane should lead us."

"Amen to that," said Hicks, twisting out his cigarette butt with his toe. Cardell slung his guitar over his shoulder and gently nestled it on the stand. He clawed through his black backpack and pulled out a baggie and a ceramic bowl. The pipe had a bust of Yoda smiling his enlightened plastic smirk.

"I think I'll pass, guys," I said. Christ, it was only four o'clock. I had to get home and have Sunday dinner with my parents after this.

"Whatchya talkin' about, man?" Cardell reprimanded. He had the look of a rock 'n' roll Gargamel, with long greasy, black hair, pale face, and beaky nose. "The only way to play music is stoned. You come up with the best shit."

"I don't know. I don't think I got stoned last night."

I hadn't, either. We had driven out to this hunting access off Union Road where Eric Jimenez and his buddies were having a bonfire. Jimenez was my lab partner in chemistry. We talk about rock 'n' roll. He digs my poetry. I dig his drawings.

Jimenez had pilfered an Erlenmeyer flask from the lab while I kept his cover. He had contrived a metal bowl that fit over the top of the flask. He had stuffed the bowl full of weed and heated up the water at the bottom of the flask over the fire. Something was supposed to happen, but it didn't.

Instead, Jimenez poked holes into the side of a beer can, and we used it as a marijuana pipe.

It was out of that Busch Light can that I smoked marijuana for the first time.

I wasn't lying, I didn't feel a damn thing. Cardell, Hicks, and Jimenez were giggling like schoolgirls. I had a couple of Busch Lights and got drunk, but the marijuana did nothing for me. What the Hell. If it doesn't get me stoned, what harm can it do?

Cardell handed me the loaded Yoda bowl.

"May the Force be with you," he said with a gag, letting out a billowing cloud. The dirty, grassy smell tickled my nostrils. I set the pipe between my lips, staring at the back of Yoda's head. Here goes. If Melissa could see me now, she'd shit bricks.

Flick.

The flame hit the wavy strains of marijuana. The weed cracked. The bud bulged out of the bowl in a red glow. My lungs were drowning in smoke the second I inhaled. It rushed back out with a wheezing gag. Orange, burning herb flew out of the pipe and onto the cracked, concrete floor. I coughed, hacked, my eyes scorching, tears swelling.

"Shit!" Hicks scolded. He stooped down on his knees and scrounged up the scattered weed.

"Sorry, dude," I panted. That sucked. My lungs burned. I limply handed the pipe over to Hicks. He stuffed the loose strands of weed back in the bowl. He put the pipe to his lips and puffed. He had thick, wrestler's arms and a blonde, near-white, crew cut shaved close. His cauliflower ears were lined with gold rings with an additional ring poking out from his eyebrow.

He handed the pipe back to Cardell.

The garage came into heightened focus.

I plopped my ass down in my drum throne. All weight was lifted from my shoulders. I tapped the snare drum.

"Heh, heh, heh."

Euphoria. Fuck yeah.

"Heh, heh."

I giggled and I tapped at the drum. Ratta-batta-tatta.

The bowl found its way back into my hands. The drumsticks rattled on the rim as I set them on the snare. I took a hit. This time I took the pipe out of my mouth before I started coughing. Baby steps.

I was swimming inside my own head. I could feel the gravity reversing between my ears. Awesome.

"You're fucking stoned, dude," laughed Cardell, once again passing the torch to me. His cackling face, wavering.

"Heh, heh, heh."

Timeless, slow motion. Was that really my hand? How did the lighter get in my other hand? All was well. I knew what to do with it. Flick, suck, cough.

"Fuck yeah, dude."

"Let's rock."

I could see the music flowing out of Cardell's guitar. I could feel it vibrating down my spine. I had an answer to every question. And Hicks knew the same. Rock 'n' roll.

Swish went the high-hat. Bam went the snare. Boom-ba-da-boom went the bass.

I don't remember playing. I don't remember starting, and I don't think we stopped.

Fuck yeah.

I was stoned as all get out and the world loved me for it.

21

BEATS AND CHEATS

December 9, 1995

The nerves pop up from within like the groundhog seeing its shadow. You never know what the damn little rodent is going to see. Do we have two weeks of winter? Is it six?

There are no nerves when I play football. It's just glee inside. The manicured grass slides under my feet like a roller rink. I'm fluid. I'm a rabbit. I can cut in and out of breaks with ease. Seven steps, hit the hash, and cut. Hands up. Form a triangle. Catch the ball.

Speaking in front of class, that's another bucket of bait. It's an exercise in dread. The words are right there on the notecards in my hand. The sweat smears the pencil marks. My hands shake. My head quivers. I hope no one notices. They notice, though.

They always notice. Story of my life. All eyes on Robert.

Playing music on stage is a different beast. Playing with the orchestra was no sweat. I got to hide in the back row, ratta-tat-tatting on the snare drum or waiting for the mustachioed music teacher Mr. Schneller to point at me so I could crash those crash cymbals loud enough to wake the dirties in the machine shop.

I enjoyed that part. All eyes on me.

Now playing with my band... Cool Veins.

We played our first show today at Rosy's. All day I was nervous, anxious, that pit in my stomach swallowing up any appetite. Once it came time to play, it was all business. You go through the ritual of setting up the drum kit. Tightening the lugs. Screwing in the cymbals. Waiting for the guitarists to tune. Playing the songs.

Bang, boom, crash. Nothing to it.

I did speed up during the break down of the first song. I got excited when we went from the quiet part to the loud part, rushing through my fill. Hicks, wearing a white tank top, flayed parachute jeans, and beanie, thumbing at his thumping bass, gave me a scowl. I fell back into the groove and kept it there for the rest of the gig. One, rat, and three, tat.

Hicks and I wove a flowing rhythm while Cardell, in his camouflage pants and red flannel, wailed away on his guitar. I was also wearing a flannel shirt. The green one I liked.

My drum set is now crumpled in the corner of Rosy's Diner in a heap, like a pile of bric-a-brac dumped from a bucket. Bay windows surround the front walls of the diner from floor to ceiling and the sunlight streams in reflecting off the snow and ice piled up in front of the window in blinding fashion.

The audience, teenage metalheads in Slayer T-shirts and combat boots, sit at round tables covered in a plastic matting. Their arms are crossed. They scowl. Nobody clapped when we finished our 30-minute set.

Rough crowd.

We are part of a day-long metal show coordinated by the owner of the used record shop down the alley off Main Street. A friend of Hicks' cousin. The only problem is we aren't a metal band. At least those who categorize such things wouldn't consider Cool Veins as metal. I guess we are grunge. We play blues progressions with fuzzy guitars and Cardell and Hicks grunt in their guttural growls.

The alternative scene of Crawford Falls huddles in small pockets on the college campus here. You can hear the slacker songs coming out of Boston and Seattle late at night on the college radio station. If I'm up late I'll slip on the headphones of my Walkman and slide the dial over to The Edge 97.5 and listen to the latest alternative tunes as I nod off to sleep.

If we were able to play in the college bars, like Slim's, we could find those alt rock pockets. Unfortunately, Hicks and Cardell are still underage. They're not allowed in the bars after 8pm.

So here we are on a sunny Saturday afternoon playing for a bunch of greasy sourpusses in Rosy's Diner. A couple of giggly sophomore girls here to see Hicks stick together like twin popsicle sticks in the back corner.

Most of these guys are from the north side of the river. Northies. The factory in town builds motor parts for one of those car manufacturers up in Detroit. Most of the factory workers live on the north side in the Crawford River flood plain.

Rosy's is on the north end of Main Street, on the south side of the river. Head west up First Atreet and you find the new residential neighborhoods where the McMansions are built for the factory engineers and university professors.

We moved there a couple a years ago from the north side after Dad got a promotion at the bank and Mom started her job at the hospital full-time. Mom's a townie here in Crawford Falls. We had a lot of the same elementary school teachers. Everyone says we have the same eyes.

Dad's from farm country. He keeps changing the town he's from. Sometimes he says, "Black Hawk." Sometimes he says, "Alton." Wherever it was, he went to Western U for college. That's when he met Mom, I guess. He was pretty antsy to build the new house. Put Jess and I in Scouts and every sports team to prove that he's a local too, or something.

Crawford Falls is one of those towns that you can't call yourself a local unless your family helped lay the bricks on Main Street. Or if you're rich. If you have money, then everybody in this town loves you. I guess that's how it is no matter where you live.

It's like Marx said, "Money is the alienated ability of mankind."

I don't need money. I have the ability, and I'm not an alien.

Anyway, I start packing my drums away in the drum bags. The trap set is a scratched-up, black Pearl custom set I bought from some kid who had it set up in his family barn out there off Union Road. He had bought it off some hair metal drummer who had to sell it after he got his girlfriend knocked up. When I found it in the barn it was covered in cobwebs and mouse spit.

I bought the whole kit and caboodle for $250 with gift money I got from my Eagle Scout ceremony. I cleaned up the toms. Polished the cymbals. Started practicing.

Now we played our first real show. This is just the beginning.

The record shop manager saunters over. He graduated a couple years ahead of us. Justin or something or other. He wears a black Judas Priest T-shirt and has dyed-yellow hair that is dark at the roots.

"Hey man, get your shit outta here," he snarls. "The other band's gotta get through here."

"Oh yeah, sorry man," I say, rushing to take apart the hi-hat stand. "How did it sound?"

"Like a Pearl Jam rip-off," he growls. He stalks off to gripe at the next band to hurry their asses up.

I am crestfallen. Then Eric Jimenez shows up out of the blue. He stops Hicks and Cardell, who are lugging their amplifiers off the stage. Jimenez is this hulking, long-haired dude that moved from, where was it, maybe Cedar Rapids I think, like last year.

The factories started hiring a bunch of Mexicans and they and their families set up shop in a trailer park on the north side. Jimenez's dad is some kind of lawyer that helps the migrant workers with their visa documents and paperwork and stuff.

Jimenez was on the football team when he first arrived, but then on his first practice the other linemen made it a game to stomp on his testes during one-on-one tackle drills. Jimenez never came back.

During science lab he taught me some cool ways to burn shit so the chemicals give off pink flames. "What's up," I say, nodding at Jimenez.

"My dudes!" hollers Jimenez clapping Cardell and Hicks on the back. "Awesome set. Totally rocked."

Cardell and Hicks nudge by him, and Jimenez wriggles over to me hovering awfully close as I zip the last bag for my bass drum.

"Who knew a preppy could rock the drums like that," he laughs with a guffaw.

"Thanks, man," I say, my heart warming up a bit.

"You smoke?" asks Jimenez. He speaks in a nasally tone like his nose is permanently stuffed.

"Smoke?" I ask.

"Yeah, herb," he says. "I'm gonna spark a bowl in my car. Wanna come."

"Ahh," I hem, and I wave him off. "No thanks. I gotta have supper with my parents."

"All good, all good," he says.

I lift my drums and shuffle over to the side door where my dad's Ford F150 is parked outside, leaving Jimenez behind. Dad let me borrow the truck so long as I fill it up with gas. He loaned me his credit card to use.

I heft my drums into the bed, and I watch Cardell and Hicks sneak into the back seat of Jimenez's vintage Cadillac.

I guess I'll just go home then.

22

A Cat From New Mexico

January 4, 1996

"You're telling me that there is nothing alive in those things?" asked Cardell, pointing at three jumping beans convulsing on the homemade brick table.

"No, dude, they're jumping for the light," said Robert, who was sitting across from him on a worn-out, plaid sofa. Hicks was sitting next to him, pounding away on an acoustic guitar.

"Are you sure?" asked Cardell, incredulous. "I thought there were little worms inside."

Cardell picked up one of the shells and watched it twitch in his hand.

"Besides," he said. "There's no light in here anyways."

The three delinquents were sitting in Hicks' basement, bundled up in blue jeans and flannel. Two lamps fitted with blacklight bulbs dimly illuminated the musty room in a neon hue. A ping-pong table sat silent in the corner, covered in a film of dust and open Playboys. The Donna D'Errico centerfold was spread out on top, her teeth beaming bright in the black light.

Two couches flanked the coffee table cobbled together with cement brick blocks and a marble slab. The Mexican bean, a beige wiggly shell the size of a pistachio, bounced off of Cardell's palm.

"Shit!" he shouted, ducking down to the ground and clawing at the shag carpet. He sat up, unsuccessful in his search for the bean.

"Hey, dude, you wanna load one more bowl before we go to Jimenez's?" Hicks asked, looking up from the guitar.

"Sure, dude," said Cardell. He dug into a sandwich baggy and stuffed a nug into his Yoda bowl.

"I think I'm good," said Robert, raising his hand in surrender.

"Come on, man. You can't give up now," said Cardell, lighting up the cherry.

"Yeah, man. Don't be a pussy," said Hicks, as he took the torch from Cardell and took a hit.

"Nah, dude. I'm seein' sideways."

"The kine bud really got ya, huh," Cardell slurred. "It's killer, man."

"I'll cash it then," said Hicks. He took a big hit off the pipe and what was left of the nug smoldered into ashes. He blew out a stream of smoke. He picked up the guitar, leaned back into the couch and with the guitar perched on his knee started strumming Alice in Chains.

"You know what really gets me?" asked Robert, cracking open his red, squinted eyes. "These fucking politicians, man. I mean, what is their job, really? I mean, the president won't say 'boo' to Hillary unless some advisor fuckin' hands him a notecard. He doesn't do shit. The guy's got no soul. No offense, Cardell."

"What?" said Cardell, perking up. "Da fuck you talking 'bout, man?"

"Yeah, President Cardell," Hicks laughed.

"Ain't my job," said Cardell, lighting up a cigarette. "I got impeached."

"I guess that's just the F-man talkin,'" said Robert, slumping back onto the couch and taking the bowl from Cardell.

"The what?" sputtered Cardell through a cloud of smoke. "I thought you voted for Billy. What the fuck are you talkin' about?"

"The F-man."

"The what-man?"

"The F-man," said Robert, straining his burning throat.

"I can never fucking hear what you're saying, dude. You mumble so fuckin' soft. Now, what did you say? The Breath-man?" Cardell shouted, shaking his hands vehemently.

"No, dude," Robert giggled, and passed the bowl. "The F-man."

"The F-man? What's that?"

"It's the reason for your being, man. That special thing inside you. It's the reason you see me out of your own eyes instead of Chad's," said Robert, rambling on. "It's the reason you hated being president, but you wouldn't be president unless you wanted to. It's the reason you tell us you hate the job, but it's also the reason you ran for the job. It's the you that you love and the you that you hate. It's the you that you show to your parents, and the you that you show us here in the basement. They're all one and the same person, but not. It's the F-man Himself."

Robert paused. His glazed eyes studied his manicured fingernails.

"It's the jealousy that you have that makes you hate someone," continued Robert, mumbling again. "You know, for some reason, you're jealous of some dude, for... for... stealing your girl... but you feel ashamed for feeling jealous. So, you hate someone and want some dumb reason to kick his ass. But... really you wanna kick your own ass."

Robert's eyes blazed and glazed.

"Speak up! Seriously dude!" shouted Cardell. "Annunciate! Fuckin' speak from your stomach!"

"That's why you're the singer and I'm the drummer," laughed Robert.

Hicks put the guitar down and lit a cigarette of his own.

"So, what you're saying," Hicks said, smoke streaming from his lips. "Is that we hate other people because of what we hate in ourselves?

"Whatever," Robert muttered, and he grabbed Hicks' guitar and laid it across his lap. "All I know is all I wanna be is a rock 'n' roll star."

Robert pounded out a few discorded chords on the strings.

"Yeah, dude," said Hicks, yanking the guitar from Robert. "When we gonna practice next?"

"We can use my garage tomorrow afternoon," said Robert, dropping his hands in innocent grievance. "My folks'll be out."

"Cool, man," said Cardell, tapping his cigarette on the edge of a clay ashtray. "Y'know, I was thinkin'. If these next few shows go good, we should seriously think about moving to L.A. after graduation."

"Fuck yeah, dude. I'd be there in a heartbeat," Robert nodded.

"I don't know if I could leave Debi," said Hicks, shaking his head. "I think this girl is cool. We might be together for a while."

"You're full of shit. I give you two months," said Cardell, laughing. "Enough time to get another girlfriend before graduation."

"No, dude, I could fall in love with her."

"Sure, you'd love her 'til you find another blonde with big tits who'll let you slobber all over 'em 'til Sunday."

"That's why we should go to California," Robert added, with a guffaw.

"No shit!" The triumvirate chuckled in chorus.

"Let's... uh... I guess we should get to Jimenez's," said Cardell, stuffing the Yoda pipe and bag of weed into the pocket of his black corduroys. They tumbled out of their seats.

"Shit," Robert cursed as something crunched under his foot.

"What?" Cardell asked.

"I just stepped on something."

Robert stooped over and inspected the floor. He picked up a crushed jumping bean.

"Whoops."

He held his prize up in the light. He brushed away the tiny shards of shell. A neon green worm writhed in his palm.

***

The emptiness. The fear of finding a reason to grow up.
A generation that has been given everything but has nowhere to go.
Kids waiting for someone to pull the trigger.

23

IT TOOK EVERYTHING

May 28, 1996

Robert eased back into his seat on the basement couch. They were again shacked up in Hicks' basement. High school graduation was fresh in the rear-view mirror. For Robert, the end of the school year couldn't come soon enough.

The constant pressure from his parents: "Why did you quit track?" "Apply for scholarships." "Get a job." "I don't like your friends." "We didn't raise you this way." "You're better than this."

His heart still ached every time he saw Melissa walking down the school hallway. He dropped all the classes they shared. He quit all the committees they had joined together. He needed an escape from the other girls jockeying for his strap.

After the graduation parties had all ended Robert finally felt like he could breathe. Summer suns dry up the muck of spring. Robert hadn't told his parents yet, but he withdrew enrollment from Western U. His writing scholarship was null and void. Shit was gonna hit the fan.

For Robert, the idea of no commitments, no pressure, no anxiety, was like lying in a grassy field looking up at the beautiful blue sky. The world was open to him, and it lighted a fire in his gut to get out and explore. To go see what he could see.

He found solace behind the drum set. The heavy sound drowned out the outside noise and bullshit. He could smoke a bowl and lose himself to the music.

More often than not, he was holed up in some garage, basement, or bedroom smoking doobies with Cardell and Hicks.

On this fine summer day, the trio were with Jimenez passing a joint around Hicks' dank basement.

"You know," said Robert, eyes baked halfway shut. "The TV has really taken over."

Hicks passed the joint to Jimenez, bypassing Robert, who was sitting next to him on the couch. Jimenez was in an easy chair, his gray poncho covered in stains. Cardell was seated in a wooden spindle chair, an acoustic guitar in his lap.

"I mean, who doesn't watch TV?" Robert continued in a foggy drawl. "I suppose I met a few people who don't, but only like two. My crazy uncle living off the grid, I suppose. But like, there are, like, two out of one million human beings that don't watch TV. It's like, everyone's opinion is based on what they watch on the tube, man. It's like, people vote for the politician they've seen on the TV the most. The idiot box."

Robert muttered the last part under his breath. Jimenez passed the joint to Robert, who continued his soliloquy.

"All anybody talks about is what they saw on TV last night. It's all that anyone has in common anymore. The world is in the hands of the producers. That's why everyone loves the internet. It's like TV, except you get to take part. You are the show. Christ, man, who really listens to anybody anymore? Who needs love anymore? What are our basic needs? Food, shelter, air, and love? The first three, are, like, self-sufficient needs. But love, we need other people to love us. It's like, with TV, and the computer, we create our own little worlds. Y'know, love becomes a self-sufficient need. Sometimes I just think about that."

"Less talk, more smoke," Hicks berated. Robert quit waving the bone around and took a drag from it.

"Yeah man," said Cardell with a wheezing chuckle. "Like, I make self-sufficient love every morning."

"Besides," chided Jimenez. "That's called the mass society theory. You're not the first one to think of that. *1984* motherfucker."

"Oh," said Robert, glumly. "Right."

"Do you guys ever wonder," asked Cardell, setting down the guitar to take his turn with the joint. "Do you ever wonder if girls, like, fantasize about you when they masturbate?"

"What?"

"Well, you know, girls masturbate. It's a given. And there isn't a single girl out there, like one single floozie in all of CF High, that I haven't fantasized about, you know, while like jerking it. It makes me think, man, that there must be some girl out there, somewhere, maybe right now even, at least one, thinking about me while fingering herself. Digging for pearls. It kind of gives me a boner. Y'know?"

"No shit."

"You know who's thinking about you right now?" asked Hicks, a devilish grin showing his two buck teeth. The rest of his face hidden by the curled bill of his cap.

"Beth Miller?"

"No," said Hicks, his grin growing wider. "Your mom."

He burst into a giggle.

"Fuck you," grumbled Cardell, picking up the guitar again.

"Play some Beatles," said Robert, in his slow drawl.

"You guys coming over this weekend?" asked Jimenez, drumming his fingers on his belly.

"What's going on?" asked Cardell, strumming the first few chords to "Blackbird."

"A party at my new house," said Jimenez, with a sour face. "I told you like a thousand times."

"Oh yeah...," said Robert with a cheesy grin. "You're house-morning party."

"Yeah, that," said Jimenez, with a grimace.

"You got a keg?" asked Hicks.

"I hope so," said Jimenez, almost forlorn. "If Bone comes through."

"Let us know when you got a keg," said Hicks.

"Yeah, yeah," said Jimenez, speeding up his finger drumming.

"Who's gonna be there?" asked Cardell.

"The usual, y'know," said Jimenez. "Linus... uh... Trav and his band..."

"Chicks, man," cursed Cardell. "Any chicks comin'?"

"Yeah!" said Jimenez, brightening up. "Yeah, man... you know Virginia? Virginia Gross? She said she's comin.'"

"Gross Vagina?" said Hicks with a chuckle.

"Shut up, dude," cursed Jimenez. "She's hot as hell. We like... we like might have a thing..."

"Just... y'know... keep yer dick clean," said Hicks, continuing his chuckle. "That thing's filled with slime. I heard she let Klink stick it in her pooper."

"Fuck you," said Jimenez, chucking a throw pillow in Hicks' direction.

"We'll see, man, we'll see," said Cardell, ignoring the scuffle. "I get off my shift at 10."

"Have you guys seen the spheres?" asked Robert, eyes blazing. "I saw 'em the other night. I was just lying in bed. I saw three spheres, rotating, all connected at a single point..."

"Don't be weird, dude," grumbled Hicks. "Keep yer shit together."

24

THE DEVIL CAN HEAR YOU KNOCKIN'

June 1, 1996

"Hey man, you got a lighter?" Cardell asked.

"Yeah, man," said Robert, reaching into his pocket, pulling out a yellow Bic lighter. He passed it to the front of the VW bus. They were cruising back to town from Alton where they had just picked up Cardell from his uncle's bar. Everyone had a shot of Jäger before leaving.

"No man. We can't use this one. It's yellow."

"What's wrong with a yellow lighter?"

"It's bad luck."

"Here. Use mine," said Hicks, who took his hand off the steering wheel to hand a blue lighter to Cardell.

"Thanks."

Cardell took a hit out of the Yoda bowl and handed the lighter back to Hicks. Then he rolled down the passenger window and chucked Robert's yellow lighter out the window. It rattled down the dark highway like Luke's lost lightsaber.

"Hey! That was mine. Christ, what are you doing?" Robert protested from the bench seat in the back. The upholstery was so worn he was basically sitting on the foam padding.

"It was yellow, man. You can't use it. Here."

Robert leaned forward and took the bowl from Cardell.

"Hicks, can I use your lighter, dude?" Robert asked, meekly.

"Yeah."

Robert graciously accepted the blue lighter and sparked the bowl. He inhaled and gagged. Smoke gushed from his mouth and filled up the body of the bus. He coughed and wiped spittle from his lips. Davis, his seat mate, so tall his poofy brown hair nearly bumped the roof of the VW bus, let out a little cough.

"That was a good hit," complimented Cardell.

"Yeah, it was," said Robert, wiping his mouth. He turned to his left. "You want a hit, Davis?"

"No thanks, man," Davis said in his low rumble.

"You sure?"

"Yeah, I'm sure."

"Aw, come on!" Hicks jeered from the driver's seat. "Davis, you never smoke anymore! Come on, just this once."

"No, I'm good. I got a forty."

To put the exclamation on his point, Davis took a swig from the 40-ounce bottle of Olde English sitting between his thighs.

"More for us then," said Hicks, and he accepted the bowl from Robert. He took a deep hit and French-curled the smoke. He passed the bowl to Cardell and put his hands back on the steering wheel. The VW bus chugged along.

"Hey man, where do you want to go?" asked Cardell as he took his turn with the bowl.

"Jimenez is having his party tonight," said Robert, taking the bowl from Cardell. He took a hit.

"Did he move into that house?" asked Hicks, taking the bowl from Robert. He took a hit.

"Yeah, tonight's his housewarming party. Remember?"

"Yeah, sure...," said Cardell, tapping the ashes out of the bowl into the flip-up console ashtray of the VW. "This thing is cashed."

"Does he have a keg?" asked Hicks, lighting up a cigarette.

"Yeah."

"How much for a cup?"

"For us? Free."

"Sounds good to me," said Cardell, tapping the cherry of his cigarette out the window. "You gonna call Debi?"

"Nah man," grumbled Hicks. "We broke up."

"Told ya," giggled Cardell.

"Hey Davis!" called out Hicks. "You wanna go to Jimmy's?"

"Nah, I don't think so. I should go home."

"Party pooper, man."

"I got church tomorrow."

"We all got church tomorrow."

"Yeah, but my church isn't in the Hill Street Deli."

"I'll say a little prayer for you," Cardell giggled.

"All right," said Hicks. "I'll drop you off."

Cardell leaned way over and dug around inside his sock. He pulled out a rolled up sandwich baggie.

"Hey, you wanna load one more?"

***

When they rolled into Jimenez's there were already guys stumbling out on the front lawn breaking chairs. A pack of kittens sat on the roof, cheering them on. There were several bare patches on the roof where there should have been shingles. The house's white siding was flaking off. The railing on the porch was ready to collapse.

The carnage of the house was a beacon of the hellbent destruction triggering the misfits to surge forward.

Cardell, Hicks, and Robert found a spot to park the VW bus further down the residential street and strolled up the front drive. Jimenez's father's pristine law office was next door. He had bought the house as a real estate investment, believing Jimenez and his friends would bother to pay rent.

"What's up fellas?" called out Hicks.

"Hey! Nothin' much," said one of the dudes, Linus, a slim ceramics dork from overseas, maybe one of the Baltic states, who was stomping on the splintered legs of a dining chair.

"Is Jimmy in there?"

"Yah, he's here somewhere."

"Cool, we're gonna go in."

"Yah, catch ya later."

"Yeah, later."

Hicks, Cardell, and Robert wandered up the sagging porch and through the front door, slapping hands with everyone they passed. A group of strung-out kids in black T-shirts and baggy jeans were gathered in the front room. The trio passed by them and into the bright kitchen.

"Hey, what's up?" It was Duke, a short, blonde kid with coke-bottle goggles who staggered into the room. A pair of Hanes briefs was elasticated around his head. "You need a beer?"

"Hey, Duke. What's with the underwear?"

"Oh, they're Bone's. Some girl put 'em on me."

"Nice. Where's the keg at?"

"In the tub. The cups 're over there."

Each of the trio collected a plastic cup and trooped into the bathroom. Bone, a meathead with wild curly hair and a USA headband was pumping the tap, a bottle of vodka in his other hand.

"What's going on?" said Bone, taking a giant swig from the bottle. "Ya need a beer?"

"Yeah, man. Fill me up," said Cardell, holding out his cup. "Who all is here?"

"Jimenez is upstairs in the black light room with some people. Uh, Tom Brighton's on leave from the Army and he and some guys are out back. I think Travis is in the basement jamming with his band. Linus and some of his acid-head friends are out front..."

"Yeah, we saw them."

"Ogre is supposed to be here after work."

"Aw, cool. I haven't partied with him in forever," said Cardell, his plastic red cup overflowing with foam. "Thanks man, I'll catch ya when I'm empty."

"Yeah, peace out, dudes."

Hicks, Cardell, and Robert climbed up a rickety stairway curtained with crêpe paper streamers sipping at their beers. The main room upstairs was engulfed in shadow and scattered with teenagers. The trio waded through the mindless chatter to the other side of the room.

They opened the door to the next room and a cloud of smoke billowed in their faces. The overhead light fixtures were fitted with black lights. The walls inside were glowing as were the fluorescent dragons postered on the wall. Jimenez was seated in a leather recliner in the corner. He was wearing a cut-off heavy metal T-shirt and cut-off cargo pants. Reclined, his belly rose like a turtle shell. He had a toothy grin. His teeth glowed green in the black light.

Two girls were sitting on a sofa pushed up against the side wall with their knees clasped together. They had barrettes pulling back their bleach-blonde hair and black eyeshadow making them look like glow-in-the-dark children of the corn.

Three guys sat in a triangle on the floor pulling tubers.

"Cardell! Chaswick! Longley! What's happening?" called out Jimenez, his grin growing bigger. "You guys find beer? All right! My men!"

"What's up, Jimmy?" They all produced their cups in a salute.

"Hey, let's go to the basement. I want to show you something," said Jimenez. He struggled to lift his massive frame out of his chair, knocking over a cup of beer in the process.

"Ah, fuck! Hey, Tom Thumb, clean that up for me, will ya?"

"Uh, sure," said one of the guys on the floor.

"Come on," said Jimenez. "This is way cool."

The triumvirate followed the hulking Jimenez, his long, black hair flowing down his back, down to the musty basement where shrouded musicians banged out a sludgy metal song on their instruments. A streaked kid with red eyeliner keyed out the drum beat on his computer.

"Fuck that," Robert muttered.

"It's back here," said Jimenez.

His wallet chain jingled as he unlocked a padlock on a door in the shadows. He swung open the rickety door and they walked into a tiny, concrete room. Robert brushed cobwebs from his face. The only contents of the windowless bomb shelter were a fluorescent light hanging low from the ceiling over a rubber tub filled with fertilized soil.

"It's my hydroponics set up," said Jimenez. "I'm going to grow my own plants, so I don't have to sell anymore."

"Wow, that's cool."

"Don't tell anyone," said Jimenez, putting a thick finger to his lips. "Don't wanna get ratted out. You three and Linus are the only ones I've shown this to."

"That's fuckin' ill, man."

"Hey, you guys lookin' for anything?"

"Sure, what do you have?"

"I measured out some eighths. They're twenty."

"Cool, man."

25

— ● —

WAR CRIMES

June 2, 1996

Debi showed up to the party after all and she and Hicks disappeared into the labyrinth of spare rooms.

Cardell was in the basement jamming with the goth band.

Robert was upstairs alone. Well, not alone. He just wasn't with his friends. He found himself in the same room where they found Jimenez before, the one where the walls were lined with fluorescent, fire-breathing dragons. Jimenez was bopping around somewhere. Robert thought he heard him shouting into a microphone from the basement.

The second-floor sin den was littered with teenagers. Some of them recent graduates. Some were younger kids whose parents didn't know where they were. Ogre sat in the easy chair smoking a cigarette. His girth filled up the chair. He gave Robert a smile and a wave. Robert waved back.

"What's up, Ogre?" he said.

"Crazy seeing you here," said Ogre with a smile, his cropped dark hair slicked to the side.

"Yeah man," said Robert. "You too."

A black rotary phone sat in the middle of the wooden floor. The cord ran the length of the floor and plugged into the wall. Linus sat cross-legged on the floor in front of the phone. Linus had a shaved, lopsided head that made his ears stick out even more. With a bulbous nose and protruding lips he looked like a Buddha that lived under the bridge.

Those lips now quivered. His nose was wet with snot.

Virginia Gross sat on the couch. The seat next to her was empty. She motioned to Robert to sit down. She was wearing jeans frayed at the cuffs and a white baby-T. She had shoulder-length brunette hair streaked with blonde highlights like a mall rat version of *Friends*.

Robert sat next to Virginia. She felt soft. Her face was shiny with makeup and Robert could see the bumps of acne underneath the smear. She had wide brown eyes and puckered, glittery pink lips.

"What's going on?" asked Robert.

"I can't believe you're here," said Virginia with a giggle.

"What do you mean?" asked Robert.

"I mean, like, you're a football star," said Virginia, again tittering, squeezing her jiggly boobs between her biceps.

"Nah," said Robert bluntly, shaking his head. "Not me, man."

"I can't believe you party," said Virginia.

"Well," said Robert, glibly. "It's summer vacation."

Robert took a sip of his beer and set the cup on the side table. He noticed that Virginia's hands were empty. She drummed her fingers lightly on her thighs.

"What's up with Linus?" Robert asked.

"He's waiting for his dad to call," said Virginia.

"What?"

"Yeah, I guess his dad is, like, supposed to call tonight."

"Where from?"

"He's, like, still in Bosnia," said Virginia. "I guess, like, Linus hasn't talked to him in two years."

"Two years?"

"Yeah, with, like, the war and all," said Virginia. "Linus doesn't know if he's alive. His grandma's gonna call, like, any minute and, like, let him know."

"Jesus," said Robert.

"Can I tell you something," said Virginia, wide-eyed, resting her fingers on Robert's bicep.

"Sure," said Robert. "I guess."

"I mean, like, do you remember we had creative writing together?" gushed Virginia. "Like, we were in the same class."

"Sure," said Robert. "I remember. I liked your story, the one about your sister."

"I can't believe you noticed me," blushed Virginia. "Like, you were the best writer in class."

"I don't know," Robert said. "Like, I was just making shit up."

"You remember that poem you read in front of class?" asked Virginia. "It was like, one and one is three."

"Abraxas is my name," said Robert. "That wasn't me. That was Cody."

"Oh," said Virginia, her grip loosening on Robert's arm.

"I read the Valentine's Day poem," said Robert. "About being alone on Valentine's Day."

"Oh, that's right," said Virginia, brightening up. She continued, "People said you were this great writer, and I was like, whatever, I mean, how can this football player be, like, a sensitive writer. But then you read your poem, and I was like, oh my God."

"Cool," said Robert. "Thanks."

"Do you still write?"

Just then the rotary phone rang. The sudden blare made every kid in the room jump. Linus quickly picked up the receiver and put it to his ear. He wiped his nose.

"Molim?" he said, his voice quaking.

The room went silent. All eyes were on Linus. He lightly nodded his head, his eyes unblinking, listening to a muffled woman's voice on the other end of the receiver.

"Dah.... Dah," said Linus. "Neh Rahzoomiyem."

Linus' face was turning maroon under the blacklight. His tear-streaked cheeks shimmered luminescent green.

"Dah," he said. "Dah.... Havahla.... Chao."

Linus slipped the receiver on top of the rotary dial. He placed his palms on his crossed knees. He stared at the phone.

"Um...," said Ogre. "How's your dad?"

Linus' bottom lip quivered. He sucked in a stream of runny snot.

"Nobody knows...," he said. "Nobody knows."

Linus dropped his head down into his lap and wrapped his fingers behind his head.

He howled. Some girls rushed in and started rubbing his back, hushing him, saying, "Everything's going to be all right."

Virginia leaned in close to Robert and whispered in his ear.

"Do you wanna go someplace more quieter?"

Robert nodded. They stood from the couch and Virginia gripped Robert's hand in hers. As Robert exited the door, Linus' wails had dimmed to a whimper. Ogre caught Robert's eye.

Ogre gave Robert a wink and a thumbs up.

Robert quietly closed the door behind him as Virginia led him down the hall.

26

TALLY HO

June 2, 1996

Robert dropped his cigarette on the wooden floor of the spare bedroom and twisted it out with his toe. He stood up and zipped his fly. He stepped out into the hallway and ran into a shirtless Jimenez.

"Hey man," said Jimenez, scratching his bare, rotund belly. "Have you seen Virginia?"

"Yeah man," said Robert, blearily. "She's in there."

"Thanks man," said Jimenez, slapping Robert on the shoulder. "I'm ready for a little play."

Jimenez entered the bedroom, and Robert reached his hand out to steady himself on the wall. Robert stumbled down the hall, giggling. In the common room, a few teenagers were passed out on the floor. Robert stepped over the bodies and found the stairwell. He wound his way down to the living room.

Cardell and Ogre were playing videos games. Hicks was playing the guitar.

"We should go," Robert said.

"Where the Hell you been?" asked Cardell, tearing his blank gaze from the flashing screen.

"We gotta bounce," said Robert, urgently.

"Stay for one more bowl," ordered Ogre, a giant of a youth with bushy, brown sideburns.

"Sure," said Robert, sitting down on the couch next to Hicks. Ogre set down his controller and reached into the breast pocket of his Tommy Bahama shirt. He pulled out a glass pipe and baggie. Cardell turned off the game.

"What time is it?" Cardell implored.

"Almost 4:30," said Robert, checking his watch.

Ogre proceeded to stuff the herb in the bowl and sparked it up. He passed it to Hicks who stopped strumming the guitar to take a hit.

The room shook as someone came pounding down the stairs. Jimenez burst into the room, his long, greasy hair flailing in the air. He spied Robert on the couch and lunged for him. Virginia, wrapped in a white sheet, rushed down the stairs after him. Jimenez wrangled Robert around the neck and slammed him to the floor.

"Motherfucker!"

Cardell, Hicks, and Virginia jumped on Jimenez's back and wrenched him free from Robert's throat. Robert pulled himself up from the floor and staggered to the front door. He stumbled outside and gasped for air as he fell off the porch and onto the front lawn. He opened his mouth, and a flood of puke splattered the grass.

Cardell and Hicks clutched Robert by the shoulders and hauled him down the street to the VW bus. They threw Robert inside the sliding door and slammed it shut. They locked the doors as they clambered up into the front seats. Jimenez was outside the bus, pounding on the windows.

"I'll kill you!" he shouted, muffled.

"Fuckin' asshole better not dent my car," Hicks grumbled as the engine roared to life. He sped away and left the half-naked Jimenez raging in the middle of the road.

"What did you do?" asked Cardell, looking back at Robert, who was lying like a sack of potatoes on the bench seat. "Did you fuck Virginia?"

"I dunno," mumbled Robert, whose face was drained white. "She asked for a massage."

"Fuckin' stud, my man!" laughed Cardell with a guffaw. "What's it like stickin' your face tween those big ol' titties?"

"Yeah man," concurred Hicks, with a chuckle, lighting up a square. "She's a tight piece of ass."

"Tell me about it," murmured Robert, sitting up. "Can I bum one of those?"

"Yeah, man."

Robert accepted the cigarette from Hicks and let him spark it up. Robert gazed out the window, red finger marks streaking around his neck. The top button of his green flannel was ripped off. The neck of his T-shirt was stretched down to his breast.

"I was thinkin'," said Robert, wistfully. "We should take the band to New York. Not L.A."

"Why's that?" asked Cardell.

"New York is where it's at. The grime. CBGB. Ramones. Dylan. Beastie Boys," said Robert, eagerly. "Like L.A., man it's not our scene man. It's all just like, coked-out beach bums. Glam shit."

"You think so?" asked Cardell. "My cousin's in New York. Might make sense."

"Why not? I'll sell the Civic. Get a little cash" said Robert. "When you think about it, the whole country is open to us. Like a blank notebook. We can write whatever the hell we want. Right now. Like, right now. We can just drive anywhere. Nothing's stopping us."

"Eyes wide on Brooklyn," said Hicks, with a smirk.

"There should be a forty under the back seat," said Cardell, lighting up his cigarette. "Crack it open."

They pulled into the driveway of Robert's parents' house just as the sun was peeking over the Iowa rooftops.

***

I lost a chunk of my brain in the speaker.

I felt my pulse, and it is getting weaker.

I wanted to make a good impression, but instead I freaked her.

I searched for my soul and found it in a beaker.

When it gets quiet the stars shine brighter.

The sun was just over the ridge, but I wasn't a fighter.

A gold ball popped, and she squeezed her legs tighter.

I wanted a smoke, but I lost my lighter.

And it goes on like this for years.

The shit stain clears, but the blood still smears.

I can only weep despite the cheers,

and nothing is cleansed with self-righteous tears.

27

Fuck Em to the Very Last Drop

June 10, 1996

They did it. They had done it. The others said they couldn't do it. They said it was crazy. Dumb. A dead end.

Still, they did it. They hit the open road. New York, look the fuck out.

But first, they cried.

On the day of departure Robert slept in until well after noon. When he woke up his mother and father were at work and his sister was at softball practice. The night before his dad had said to him, "I guess you're leaving tomorrow. We'll probably be seeing you soon enough."

His mother lingered outside his bedroom door, hands clutching the belt of her robe, face pinched. "Good night, Robert," she said. Then she was gone.

Robert spent the night filling an olive green, Army duffel bag he bought at the consignment store with underwear, T-shirts, jeans, flannel, socks, and notebooks and pens and drumsticks. That afternoon, on top of the duffel bag, Robert found an envelope. His name was written in pink marker.

It was a card from Jess, his sister.

It said, "Robert, I love you and I am so proud of you. You are the best big brother. I will miss you so much. I know you will be a big rock star in NYC. Love, Jess."

Robert broke down in ugly rolling sobs.

Finally, he hefted the duffel bag in one hand and under the other arm he carried a conga drum his grandpa had bought for him for high school graduation.

When Hicks pulled up in the driveway, Robert dumped everything in the cargo hold of the VW bus. Cardell and Hicks both had red faces, puffy eyes. They drove in silence until they reached the Mississippi River.

Finally, the weed and rock music mellowed the atmosphere inside the VW bus.

"You know what it is?" asked Robert, from the back of the bus. The smoky van reeked of skunky bud. Robert handed the joint up to Cardell, who was in his usual shotgun seat. Hicks was driving as the bus cruised down I-80, the dark of night covering the windows. The thumping bass line of Orbital was rattling the VW.

"What is it?" asked Cardell, shouting over the music.

"America is dying!"

"America is dying?!" Cardell shouted again, taking a hit off the roach, and passing the bone to Hicks.

"Yeah, dude. It's not going to last much longer."

"You don't think so?!"

"Nuh-uh. Its fate is sealed," said Robert, his voice straining over the music. "America is going down just like Rome!"

"Rome was different, dude," said Hicks, passing the joint back over the seat.

"No dude," said Robert. "Rome was the king of the world, an' they got too powerful. America's the same. America is getting way to powerful. We should have listened to George Washington!"

"What did he say?" asked Cardell.

"Washington told the country not to mess around with other countries. Keep our nose in our own affairs an' shit. Y'know, not give help to other countries, and don't ask for help. America should have listened to George, and just well left enough alone. With Vietnam, Iraq, Nicaragua, we've sunk ourselves deep in the muck and nobody's gonna help us out. Just gonna let us sink."

"But we were helping other countries. Other people," said Cardell. "They would be screwed if we didn't save their asses."

"Yeah," said Robert. "But being Americans we had to add a catch."

"What catch?"

"Yeah, dude, the catch is the American dollar," said Robert. "If we're gonna help ya, then ya better pledge allegiance to the American dollar, y'know. An' it made the other countries, the people we helped, resent us. I mean, the only reason we gotta worry about nuclear war is cuz we were the ones who dropped the bomb. It's like football, man, like, if you crack back block a DB so the running back can score a touchdown, you better bet your ass you now got a target on your back. That's how I got a fucking concussion."

"What are you talking about?"

"We got too many bombs man," said Robert. "Why do we need so many bombs?"

"'Cause, dude, Russia man," said Cardell. "We gotta defend ourselves."

"With so many bombs?" continued Robert. "Look at my uncle. He's got a stockpile of assault rifles in his basement. Who's he gotta defend himself from? The goddamn Russkies aren't gonna attack Iowa. The only person he's gonna use those weapons on are his neighbors, or his own fuckin' family. He's got an itchy trigger finger, man, and one of these days, he's gonna blow away someone, and it ain't gonna be Russkies. Just like America. America's gonna blow its own brains out."

"Who's gonna pull the trigger?" asked Hicks.

"We are," Hicks mumbled, with a smirk. "The trigger generation."

"I mean, come on you guys, Russia was a threat man," argued Cardell. "You saw *Red Dawn*. Fuckin' commies."

"Really, though, what kind of threat were they? We were fighting over communism, a frame of mind, not a border, or six billion tortured, innocent people. In the Cold War, we were the bad guys. We were fighting against freedom of expression, fighting against free thought. Y'know, for a country that has a set of rules for freedom, we sure don't allow much freedom outside our own country. Fuckin' hypocrites."

"But dude, the fuckin' commies were mowing down their citizens with machine guns just for trying to leave Russia or East Germany or whatever," said Cardell. "The communists got no souls, man. They're the enemy. And we defeated the enemy."

"That's my point," said Robert, shaking his hands. "My point is that Americans were the ones to topple communism, to topple the Wall, so that we could take over the Soviet Union. I mean, the Russkies are almost as bad off now as they were before the Wall came down. They're all fuckin' waiting in line for two hours for a Big Mac that they've been saving up for for two months. American corporations are trying their damndest to take control of foreign countries. If America hadn't stomped out communism, some heroic revolutionary would have done it, brought pride to Russia, and set them straight. People can stand oppression for only so long. Instead of praising their own national hero, they have to answer to Coke and Pepsi. Instead of Vlad Lenin they gotta praise Ray Kroc. Follow our rules. The American way is the only way. And the foreigners resent us for it."

"What can they do? We're too powerful."

"Yeah, but we're getting weaker, and they are starting to catch up," Robert said. "Now that America has gained almost total power, we still want more. Americans are getting hungry and turning on themselves. It's everyone for themself. No one trusts their neighbors anymore. No one trusts the government anymore. When America is attacked, we won't have the patriotic pride to defend our country. I don't see us going down in my lifetime, but I give us a couple more centuries. We're slowly imploding, and we're going to get caught, just like deer in headlights."

"And how do you propose we stop this?"

"I don't know. How do you stop the F-man?"

"Now you're fuckin' losin' me," said Cardell. He stuffed the roach into a glass pipe. Robert blearily eyed the clock. It read 4:31.

"Shit, the sun's gonna be up soon," he said.

The eastern skies were already waking up, stretching out fingers of light over the plains of Ohio. They finished the bowl and cranked the music even louder.

28

— ◆ —

BILLY FUCKS GOATS

June 11, 1996

"Hey dude, can you spot me a square?" asked Hicks.

"Why don't we smoke a bone instead?" asked Robert, glancing sideways at Hicks. They were cruising at 75 down Highway 80 in the rusted red 1979 VW bus. Robert was driving this time. Cardell was snoozing in the back seat. The early morning interstate was deserted. The heart of America zoomed by on all sides.

"Sure, dude," said Hicks, his voice groggy. "You got the zig zags?"

"Yeah," said Robert digging into his jeans pocket, one hand on the wheel. "Wait, I guess I don't. Cardell must have 'em."

Hicks looked back at Cardell, who was splayed out on the bench seat.

"Hey Cardell!" Hicks shouted. He reached back and smacked Cardell on the knee. "Wake up!"

"What the hell was that for?" mumbled Cardell as he stirred, rubbing his knee.

"We need papers," hollered Hicks.

"Well get them then," mumbled Cardell. He dropped his head and dozed off again. Strands of his long black hair hung over his pasty face.

"Get up, shithead!" shouted Hicks. He leaned into the back seat and grabbed Cardell by the shirt collar. "We need the fucking papers!"

Cardell blinked open his eyes and swiped aside his greasy hair.

"What do you want?" he asked with a grimace.

"The papers!" Robert and Hicks shouted in chorus.

"I don't have 'em," hissed Cardell. He leaned his head back and drifted off.

"Godammit, stupid motherfucker," Hicks muttered, and he jammed his hand down the front of Cardell's pants.

"What the fuck?!" shouted Cardell, jerking forward, clutching his crotch. He careened into the front seat console, scowling.

"What the hell was that for?" Cardell ordered, indignantly.

"Give me the fucking papers!" barked Hicks.

"Where are they?"

"Check your pockets!"

They were both barking at each other like embattled sea lions.

"Jesus Christ, there are better ways to fuckin' wake someone up," Cardell mumbled, searching the pockets of his cutoff camouflage pants. "What time is it anyway?"

"11:15," Robert answered.

"Where the hell are we?"

"In the middle of Pennsylvania," Robert answered again.

"How much longer til we get there?"

"A good five hours."

"Shit," mumbled Cardell, as he continued to search the button-up pockets on his thighs. "Well, I don't have your fucking... oh wait. Here they are."

Cardell pulled a flat, orange package out of his pocket and handed it forward. Hicks took it from him with a scowl.

"It's about time," grumbled Hicks, pulling out a translucent, white square.

"Don't bother me again until lunch fucking faggots," growled Cardell, dropping his head back down and instantly falling asleep.

Hicks reached under his seat and pulled out a red Altoids tin. He opened it and pulled out a rolled-up baggy of weed. He also took out a cigarette roller, which looked like two spools of a miniature conveyer belt. He laid the paper on top of the roller and pressed it between the two spools. Then he stuffed it with a pinch of weed. He smacked his lips and proceeded to roll a joint.

"That roller comes in handy," said Robert. His eyes were locked on the highway.

"I dunno," said Hicks, pulling out the tightly wound spliff. "There's something about, like, rolling a joint with your own hands. Like putting a part of yerself in it, y'know."

"I know what you mean," said Robert. "But this roller is so easy. Rolls a clean, hard bone. Just like a cigarette."

"Yeah, sure," said Hicks, inspecting the J. "Who got you this?"

"Jimenez," said Robert. "It was a going away present."

"Didn't think you were friendly."

"Well, you know," stammered Robert. "After we won Battle of the Bands he, like, started to be cool again."

"We fuckin' kicked ass," said Hicks matter-of-factly, sparking up the joint.

"Yeah, I mean, it's no use fighting over girls," said Robert, taking the joint. "There are plenty for everyone."

"Virginia is a slut," said Hicks. "Everyone's had a piece."

"Have you?" asked Robert, blowing out a stream of smoke.

"Yeah, sure, couple a weeks ago," said Hicks. "Like, two days 'fore you nailed 'er."

"No shit," mumbled Robert. "She is a whore."

"Klink put it in her ass," replied Hicks.

"No shit. That's what you said," said Robert. His face took a turn of pale. "She was my first."

"Somebody's gotta be first," smiled Hicks. "Worry more 'bout the clap than breaking your wee little purity pledge."

"It was an abstinence promise," said Robert, taking a hit off the joint. "And I should be worried about where the hell we're going. Can you check the map for me?"

"What'm I looking for?" asked Hicks, taking a map out of the glove compartment and unfolding it.

"Does it show rest areas?" asked Robert. "I need to stretch my legs."

"Nope. None," said Hicks, perusing the map spread out over his lap while inhaling on the joint. "You know we need one of those computer maps. You know, on the computer net, right. You just, like, type where yer goin' and it just, like, gives you directions. My cousin did it. It was way cool."

"You know what scientists are making now?" asked Robert quizzically. "They're making flying cars just like in *Back to the Future Two*."

"No shit," said Hicks, exhaling.

"Yeah," said Robert, taking the joint. "But you know what really scares me?"

"What?"

"Cloning," said Robert, knowingly. "You know some dumb motherfucker with a Fisher Price chemistry set is going to clone a human."

"What da fuck," said Hicks. "My cousin told me they already cloned sheep and, like, cows and shit."

"Yeah," said Robert. "It's only a matter of time before someone tries to clone people. But you know what? I don't think cloning a human is even possible."

"What? How the fuck not?" asked Hicks. "They got the technology, dude. Like, what's different between fucking livestock and people, man?"

"It's different," said Robert. "There is a communication barrier. Like, a cloned sheep could be a homicidal maniac, and we'd never even know it. Hooves can't hold knives, man. And like, sheep don't really have a soul to begin with. Humans have souls."

"You're saying, like, a sheep doesn't have a soul?"

"Like," said Robert. "People have this ultimate desire to become God. I mean, we created computers so that we can do God-like acts. Like, break the sound barrier. Send astronauts to Mars. Or create people in a laboratory. And it's the human soul that drives us to do this."

Robert handed the bone to Hicks.

"Wait wait wait," said Hicks. "My dog most def has a soul. Don't even be going there."

"I'm just saying cloning is the line that humans would finally cross to make themselves Gods," said Robert, emphatically. "Only, we aren't gods. Remember the Tower of Babel? The people built it so they could be closer to God, only

God made them speak different languages so they couldn't communicate with each other."

"Like, I'm tryin' ta follow, really this time," said Hicks, drawing it out. "So, you're sayin' God's gonna punish us for cloning?"

Hicks passed the roach to Robert.

"Possibly," Robert answered. "I think that cloning just takes one more step to proving that God does not exist. It creates a disturbance in the Force. What good does cloning do for us anyway? What's wrong with the Biblical way of making babies? Why're we always trying to update things. Why we gotta mess with God?"

"Clones'd come in handy for extra body parts," said Hicks, and he dropped the dead roach into the ashtray.

"I suppose," said Robert, numbly.

The sound of the whirring highway and the Stick-up Nickel song on the radio filled the van.

"There's a gas station," said Robert. "I could use a coffee."

He eased off the gas pedal and rolled onto the off-ramp.

29

'Nothing's Gonna Chain My World'

June 18, 1996

An old Oriental man lounged, poised behind his shop counter. This bodega had been his home for most of his lifetime. Shelves full of household products, musty from inactivity, sheltered him from the tragedy of the modern world outside. He flicked at the fly landing on his elbow.

The ancient bell chimed miserably as the gate to his fortress swung open. A rustic farm boy, a weary wanderer, too old for his age, stepped in and glanced around the claustrophobic shop. His jeans were worn white at the knees. The tattered sleeves of a flannel shirt flopped around his wrists.

The red-headed boy hovered by the newspaper stand. He slid a copy of *The New York Times* under his arm. He trudged to the counter under the gaze of the wary keeper.

"That all?" asked the man, shifting his stance.

"A book of matches, please," said the boy. His accent was pure American, no twang, no drawl, no bite, no lisp. He flashed a glance at the old man, revealing a burning intensity hidden by his loping gait.

"Fifty cent."

The clunky register went bing and the ring resonated through the barren store. The boy rummaged in his pockets and pulled out a handful of change. He dug out a quarter, two dimes, and a nickel. A penny dropped to the floor and rolled under the counter. The boy watched it in defeat. He set the correct change on the speckled counter. He tucked the paper under his arm and returned his excess bounty to his pocket.

"Thanks," he said.

Quietly, the boy turned and ambled to the front of the store. He stopped to consider the "help wanted" sign attached to the door window.

"Are you hiring?" asked the boy.

"Start tomorrow?" asked the man, the nest of white hair bobbing on his brow.

"Sure," said the boy leaning into the door.

"6am," said the old man.

"OK," said the boy. "See you then."

The bell chimed hollowly as he left. Outside, a car honked. The shopkeeper leaned against the counter. A cockroach sped across the splotchy, yellowed, tiled floor. The man reached for a can of spray.

Another car bleated in futility outside on the streets of New York City.

30

STRUGGLING WITHIN

WHAT WAS IT THE CYCLOPS SAW?

July 23, 1996

Why can't I shit?

Robert squeezed his cheeks and clenched his fists and grunted. The white walls of the gas station bathroom closed in on him. The corners where the floor met the walls were coated in black mildew. The plunger under the cracked porcelain sink had a film of green mold at the tip.

Robert's red notebook was open on his bare legs. Dark red hair follicles streaked his pasty white chicken thighs. A cockroach scurried under the door.

Shit, this place is a dump.

Robert unclenched and held his head in his hands. He sighed and closed the notebook. He tucked his black rolling pen in the copper binders.

I can't think of anything to write. This sucks.

He could feel the shit lumped up in his bladder, curdling, aching to come out, but every time he strained the stress on his sphincter stabbed at his abdomen.

Ever since I got here. Nothing will come out.

Robert, Cardell, and Hicks had been in New York for two weeks. The VW was overheating and spewing steam when they hit the end of I-80 in Teaneck. They found a Walmart parking lot and let the VW rest while they loaded up on cigarettes and pop. After two days the Walmart security guard chased them away and ever since then they had been couch-hopping with the VW van, finding rest stops and abandoned parking lots where they could catch a few hours of sleep.

Robert didn't have a place to live, but he had a job. Every Monday through Thursday at 1am Cardell and Hicks drove him through the Lincoln Tunnel and dropped him off at the bodega in Hell's Kitchen where he hid behind the counter all night.

Robert unrolled two squares of sandpaper-like toilet paper and folded them neatly. He reached under his sweat-soaked crotch and scraped out his hole. He examined the crumpled tissue for shit. It was clean. Robert dropped it in the bowl and rested his chin on his hands.

I wonder what Melissa's doing.

She was shacked up with that asshole Kyle Sommers upstate at Cornell. Pre-law. Fucking Kyle Sommers. They were in Boy Scouts together. Sommers was like a Life Scout when Robert was but a Tenderfoot. Robert's first Boy Scout excursion was a sports overnighter at the Y. They stayed up all night playing basketball and foosball. Robert and Keith and Cody and them were playing around in the racquetball court, bouncing those blue rubber balls off the walls like atoms in a Dixie cup.

There was a knock on the door. Those little white doors had a peephole, but apparently the Y was too cheap to fill the peepholes with glass. Robert peered inside the peephole to see who it was it. It was Kyle Sommers. Sommers hocked a loogy into the peephole, and right into Robert's eye.

Fucking asshole.

Another cockroach skittered over the filmy, tiled bathroom floor, this one closer to Robert's foot.

Jesus Christ what the fuck am I doing here? Robert thought, his internal dialogue on overdrive. *I got to be at work in twenty minutes. My ass is sore and red from this fucking stool. Cardell and Hicks are out in the parking lot, passed out in the VW. I gotta wake them up to drive me to work. Then they'll just park and toke up in Central Park or something. And here I am, not shitting. I'm gonna be late and Mr. Wang's gonna go on and on. 'The second-best time is now,' he'd say, whatever that means.*

The customers are like cartoon characters. You got Zippy the gang banger getting his Philly blunts and Crabtree the stumbling drunk waiting for the clock to strike 6am so he can get that first sip of Magnum on his lips.

Mr. Wang kept a corroded baseball bat under the counter. Robert always kept one hand on its hilt.

Oh God, then there was that señorita that came in yesterday. She needed to buy breath mints. She was asking me all these questions about the best ones. Like, should she get the Tic Tacs, or the Altoids, and what are the Mentos like. Like I knew. But she didn't care. I didn't care. I was just sad when she finally picked one and left.

Her tits were perfectly round. The outline of her nipples ever so slightly protruding through her tank top. That plump ass, tearing at the seams of her spandex mini skirt, swaying as she floated to the counter. And the way she fluttered those chocolate eyes.

She wanted it.

Robert's penis tightened slightly and swelled with blood. He stroked it gently, then wrapped his fingers around his warm dick. His foreskin stretched taut. Paquita Maria Consuela Sanchez appeared in his mind, and she lowered the straps of her tank top slowly down her shoulders. Robert imagined himself massaging her giant breasts, caressing his cheek and his lips over her perfect brown nipples.

He gripped his cock even tighter, slowly jerking it up and down. He rested his back against the hard toilet tank and tilted his head. His penis was a rock in his hand. He imagined himself licking her neck and ramming it into her tight vagina.

Rocking, swaying, thighs, butt-ox, a Latin lover loving like no other. Robert's hand jerked faster and he squinted his eyes. The señorita moaned with Robert and cum squirted all over his hand and thighs. He exhaled a giant sigh as his pelvis gyrated.

He released his sloppy dick and a strand of white goo clung to his forefinger. It broke and Robert unraveled a wad of toilet paper and wiped his hands. He swabbed his softened member with the scratchy toilet paper. He polished off a drop of jizz from his knee.

Robert stood. He pulled up his jeans and buttoned them. Robert ran the faucet and washed his hands in the trickle of water. He fixed his hair in the smeared mirror. He unlocked the deadbolt on the door and walked out of the rest stop bathroom. He saw the VW bus parked under a tree. The night was black. He was somewhere in New Jersey.

The Big Apple awaited.

31

The Stars Are Shining Brighter Somewhere Else

August 15, 1996

Robert woke up to a sharp pain in his lower lumbar region.

Where am I? He thought. His head was swimming from the session the night before. *That's right. New York.*

He was tucked in a ball on the bench seat of the VW bus. Cardell and Hicks were passed out, reclined in the front seats. Robert looked at his watch. 10:30. He laid his head down and pulled his sleeping bag up to his chin.

"What am I doing?" he moaned.

His eyes were sore. Had he been crying last night? He caught a whiff of the stench of pot and cigarette smoke and B.O. that clung to the interior of the van. He struggled to keep the bile down in his stomach.

Robert slid open the cargo door and crawled out of the sleeping bag. He still had his shoes on. He stumbled out into the parking lot. They were parked at a rest stop along the highway somewhere in New Jersey. It might have been Connecticut. They switched it up every night. Didn't wanna draw attention.

A couple of semis shared the cement campground with them. Robert shook to his feet and made his way to the ditch, swishing through the overgrown weeds. He unzipped his jeans and lowered his drawers to relieve himself. He was supposed to be at work. Robert didn't care.

"Oh God, I feel like shit," he mumbled.

After shaking, and zipping up, Robert returned to the van. He couldn't go inside, or he would puke. He sat on the edge of the sliding door and lit up a smoke. Cardell's coughing jerked him from his trance.

"What time is it?" asked Cardell, stretching in the passenger seat and rubbing his sleepy eyes.

"Almost eleven," said Robert.

"Man, it's late," said Cardell, with a giant yawn. "We should get moving if we're gonna get anything done. I could use a shower. We should go back to that campground and use theirs."

"Yeah."

"We should load a bowl," said Cardell, scratching his sides. "Do you have the weed?"

"No," Robert said, after searching his pockets.

"Here, I have it," said Hicks, lifting his mussed head in the reclined driver's seat. He produced a baggy from his sock. He proceeded to stuff the stringy herb into a ceramic pipe.

"Know what I miss," Cardell asked, and hocked up a loogie. He rolled down the window and spat. "Saturday morning cartoons, man. All they show anymore are dumb shows. I miss *The Smurfs* and *Gummy Bears*. They don't show any good cartoons anymore. Kids today are missing out."

"Yeah, right," Hicks chuckled. "Remember *G.I. Joe*?"

"That wasn't on Saturday morning, dude," chastised Cardell. "That was on after school."

"But it was a cool cartoon."

"Yeah, it was," said Cardell, nodding. "I had, like, every single one of their toys."

"Me too," said Hicks, taking a hit and passing the bowl to Cardell.

"Did you ever have a wet banana?" asked Cardell, taking his hit.

"Yeah man, they were fun as hell," replied Hicks.

"Yeah, but I always slid off, and like, skinned myself on the grass," said Cardell with a guffaw.

He looked back at Robert.

"Hey, what's the matter with you?" asked Cardell, twisting around in his seat and holding the bowl out to Robert. "You sick or something?"

Robert was shaking his head.

"I feel like shit," he said.

"Last night was rough, wasn't it," said Cardell, still holding out the bowl.

"We only drank a few forties. Smoked a couple a bones," said Hicks. "Wasn't that bad ya pussies."

Hicks bypassed Robert and took the bowl from Cardell, taking a big rip.

"I don't think I can take this anymore," said Robert. He stretched on his back on the carpeted floor of the van. He could feel the grunge and dirt embedded in the carpet poking him in the back.

"What do you mean," asked Cardell, exhaling a cloud of smoke.

"I gotta go," said Robert, his heart was thumping. "I gotta go home."

"Home? No way, man," said Cardell, his voice raspy from the smoke still clogged in his throat. "You can't go. This is it. There's no turning back."

"Forward ho," said Hicks glibly, pointing two fingers like a pistol in the direction of the windshield.

Robert stared at the ceiling. The two boys in the front seat swiveled around to look at him.

"I'm going crazy," said Robert, hectically. "I can't think straight. Every day is just a blur."

"Yeah," said Hicks. "But it's fun."

"No man. I hate it," said Robert. "I hate it with all my heart."

Tears began to well in Robert's cracked eyes.

"Come on," cried out Cardell, hacking a cough, his eyes bugged out. "Soon as we get rollin', we'll be set."

"We're not rollin' anywhere," cried Robert. "We haven't gotten anywhere since we got here."

Robert sat up.

"Chill out, dude. We'll get there," said Hicks, calmly, offering Robert the pipe. "Here, take a hit."

"No man, we're not even close," said Robert. He got out of the van and paced in front of the open cargo door. "We just keep getting dicked around by managers and landlords. I work four red eye shifts at the fucking Kum Fu Go makin' fuckin' four bucks an hour. It's not close man, not close at all. I just, like, gotta cut my losses and get home before this gets anymore fucked."

Hicks and Cardell climbed out of the van from their respective doors. The doors slammed.

"It just takes time," exclaimed Cardell, confronting Robert. "Roll with the punches, man. Our break is comin'."

"I can't take it," said Robert, chest heaving. "I'm goin' crazy. All I ever think about is how good everything used to be. I should just go home. Let my parents pay for school. Watch fucking Saturday morning cartoons."

"What about the band?" asked Cardell. The three boys were a grungy triangle in the middle of a New Jersey parking lot. "We just gotta get our tape out. We get it in the hands of the right dude, and we're rock stars. Rock 'n' roll, man."

"How are we rock stars?" Robert asked, incredulously. "All we got is an acoustic guitar, Hicks' bass, and a fuckin' conga drum."

"We just gotta get settled," said Cardell in his most soothing voice. "We'll get your drum set and my amplifier sent out. My brother's gonna drive out here soon as we got a pad to crash in. Like, we'll be playin' shows before summer's over."

"Nah man," said Robert, shaking his shaggy head. "I gotta get out of here."

He climbed into the van and retrieved his Army duffel bag from the back cargo area. He scrambled back out and shoved his way past Hicks and Cardell.

"Where are you goin'?" Cardell called out. "Come on, man. Quit flippin' out."

Cardell caught up to Robert and grabbed his shoulder. Robert shook him off and strode towards the highway.

"I don't know," called out Robert. "I just gotta go. The bus stop, maybe."

The last part trailed off as Robert stumbled in the gravel. Hicks and Cardell watched him.

Robert trudged on along the shoulder of the highway in a delusional trance. He didn't bother to stick his thumb out to passing cars.

Everything will be all right, he thought to himself. *I just gotta get home. Where is the F-man now?*

After about fifteen minutes Cardell and Hicks pulled up alongside Robert in the chugging VW van. Robert climbed in the cargo door and threw his duffel bag in the back. They drove him to the bus depot in silence.

32

CRADLE AND ALL

August 17, 1996

"Please leave a message after the beep."

Beep

Robert hung up the phone and slung his Army duffel bag over his shoulder. Head down, he paced in the bus terminal.

"Excuse me," he said meekly, apologizing to a glowering lady in a tweed business dress. Robert rode down an escalator and walked out of a sliding door. A line of taxi cabs and buses were waiting for passengers. Robert lit a cigarette and continued his agitated wandering.

After three puffs he tossed the full butt into the gutter and strode back into the bus station. With the change in his pocket, he bought a soda at a snack stand. He sat on the nearest empty bench. He slurped half of the Coke. He wandered back over to the snack stand and threw the half-empty can in the trash.

Then Robert hustled back over to the pay phone. He fumbled through his change and plopped in a quarter. He again dialed a number. Someone picked up this time.

"Hi, Mom. It's Robert."

"Hi, Honey. How's it going?"

"Where have you been? I've been calling for an hour and a half."

"We were out shopping. Why, what's wrong?"

"Um..."

"Robert, what's the matter? Where are you?"

His mother's voice rose an octave.

"I'm in St. Louis."

"St. Louis? Why on Earth are you in St. Louis?"

Robert choked. He couldn't force the words out. He wiped his eyes and turned to face the wall.

"What's the matter?" asked his mother. "Are you crying?"

"Is Dad there?" Robert said in a hoarse whisper.

"Yeah, he's right here."

"Can I talk to him?"

"Yeah, sure. Here he is."

There was a brief pause. Robert could hear his parents' concerned voices, muffled, conferring with each other.

"Robert," said his dad, coming in through the receiver. "What's wrong?"

"I'm coming home, Dad."

"Why? What's the matter?"

"Nothing," Robert said, choking, wracking out a sob, then holding it in. "Nothing's wrong. I just want to come home."

"Well, okay. Where are you?"

"St. Louis."

"How did you get there?"

"A bus."

"Do you need something?"

"I'm broke. Someone stole my wallet... and my ticket."

Robert was beginning to preserve his control.

"So, what do you want me to do?" his dad asked.

"I was wondering, er, I was hoping you could wire me fifty bucks so I can catch a bus the rest of the way."

"Now, we talked about this before..."

"It's just fifty dollars, Dad. I can pay you back in a couple of weeks."

"We had an agreement. When you decided to leave... you're on your own. Your mother and I aren't going to help you out. If you want to be a grown-up, you have to take responsibility."

"What am I supposed to do? I'm flat broke! I've... I've been robbed. I have nowhere to sleep tonight!"

Robert's voice was shrill.

"Tough," said his father, sternly. "It was your decision. You decided not to go to school. You decided to move out with those idiots. You can decide for yourself what to do next. You're smart. You'll figure something out."

"Fine! Be that way!"

Robert slammed down the receiver. He looked around to see if anyone had been watching. His face was burning. His eyes welled with teardrops. He couldn't stop trembling. Robert went back outside and lit a cigarette. He tossed it aside without inhaling any nicotine. Inside the St. Louis Bus Station, he sat back down on the bench and stared at the floor. Eventually he laid over on the bench and dozed off.

When he woke up, a twinge of pain ran down his spine. The sun was setting. He left the bus station and walked until he ended up at a doughnut shop. He spent his last seventy-five cents on a cup of coffee.

He didn't touch it.

33

BUTTERNUT FINGERS LIKE TO GLOW

August 19, 1996

"Welcome to Iowa," read the giant white sign. The Hawkeye state. Iowa, you make me smile.

For Reverend Brewer crossing the border from Missouri to Iowa was like crossing the River Jordan. The luscious green Iowa cornfields waved gently in the twilight breeze. The pastures were filled with brown and white cows leisurely chewing on their cud. Some cows slept on this humid, August evening.

The pace was certainly slower here. Of course, not as slow as Minnesota. Minnesotans were nearly comatose. This man, Robert Longley, was an Iowan through and through. No doubt. Slow, graceful, purposeful movements. Didn't waste any energy. Sharp, observant, patient. If he didn't grow up on a farm, his parents did. He was sleeping now. Oh, maybe not. His homing device must be going off. Home is where the heart is.

"Where are we?" Robert yawned.

"We just entered Iowa," said Reverend Brewer. "About an hour to Des Moines."

"Oh."

"Do you live in Crawford Falls?"

Robert stared blankly at the windshield, pondering the simple question.

"Yeah, I guess so," he finally said.

"Do you have family there?"

"Yeah, I grew up there."

"There's a university there, right?"

"Yeah, Western Iowa."

"Are you in school?"

"No. I'm not smart enough."

"I don't believe that," snorted Reverend Brewer. "What are you doing instead?"

"Nothing."

The car was silent except for the occasional, methodical bump in the road. The reverend had turned off the radio after his station lost frequency.

"How old are you, anyway?" Reverend Brewer asked.

"Nineteen in a couple weeks."

"So, you have been out of school for a year now?"

"No, I graduated this spring. My parents held me back a year. I had this ear thing," said Robert, pointing at his right ear. "Now I'm holding myself back a year."

"Do you work?" asked Reverend Brewer.

"Yes... I mean, no," said Robert. "I guess I gotta find a job."

The sun had disappeared now, leaving a cuticle of pink light in its wake. It was a gorgeous night.

"So, what was going on in St. Louis?" Reverend Brewer asked. Silence did not suit the reverend. Robert once again struggled for an answer.

"I'm on my way home from New York," he finally mumbled.

"That's quite a ways. What were you doing there?"

"Trying to be a rock star," Robert said, again in a low mumble, as if talking into the collar of his flannel.

Reverend Brewer chuckled, then abruptly halted, finding the sullen look on Robert's face.

"Didn't quite pan out, huh?" said Reverend Brewer.

"Not yet anyway."

"What... do you play in a band?" Reverend Brewer asked, keeping his voice upbeat.

"I guess not anymore," said Robert, letting out a choked breath.

"Being a rock star isn't as easy as it seems," said Reverend Brewer, his voice getting firm, yet friendly. "Believe it or not, I once had aspirations of rock stardom. I mean, rock 'n' roll wasn't my thing, but I loved soul, R&B, anything from Stax Records. I played double bass in a big band in college. Man was it fun. We were good, too. But after a while, it gets to be like a job. If you want to succeed, you have to be better than everybody else, and you have to want it more than everybody else, which means you have to put in more time than everybody else. Practice, practice, practice. Ultimately, my devotion was to the Lord, not stardom... or practice. It just made more sense to join the seminary rather than twirl the bass for pennies. Turns out I'm not too bad at this. But I hope you find your sign, your calling. Because you're a bright, young man, and you have a lot to offer. Just find whatever it is that you are looking for. It will come when you least expect it."

"The F-man Himself," Robert mumbled with an exhale.

"Excuse me?"

"Nothin'."

"Do you know what Frank Sinatra said the secret to success is?" asked Reverend Brewer.

"What's that?"

"Never let them see you coming."

"I kinda like what Bob Marley said," said Robert.

"What's that?" asked Reverend Brewer.

"Everything's gonna be all right," said Robert, and then mumbled, "The F-man Himself."

34

"CAST IRON FENCES"

August 25, 1996

Cardell cracked his eyes open. He pawed at them with his fists. A box fan was balancing on the sill of the open window, clamped down by the window frame. It whirred and rattled away, protecting Cardell from the tepid NYC summer weather attempting to invade the apartment.

He was lying on the scratchy couch with the big dip in the cushion. They had rescued it from the sidewalk below on the morning of trash day. Cardell rolled over, his eyes open, to find the constricted living room. The walls were covered in lemon yellow wallpaper. Empty Rolling Rock bottles were scattered around the room on various flat resting spots, some half-full. Others were tipped over, drooling onto the waxy, hardwood floor.

Cardell realized he was still wearing his slacks and polo shirt from the day before.

Gene was sleeping on a cot in the corner. The screen of a 24-inch JC Penney TV was blue. Cardell must have fallen asleep watching a movie. What movie? The TV's speaker was buzzing out a tune. He found the remote control on the floor next to the couch and turned off the TV.

Cardell sat up and rubbed his eyes again. His head felt numb, which meant he was due for a migraine later. His guitar was leaning against the armrest of the couch. He gripped it by the neck and tucked the body under his armpit.

He found a blue Fender pick in his pocket and strummed out a G chord. Then he progressed to a C. Cardell twisted the tuning knobs to a drop D. His long, thin fingers nimbly sprayed across the strings. Hicks, wearing baggy dress of blue jeans and a white tank top, ambled into the room from the adjacent bathroom.

"What're you doing?" Hicks asked. He sat down on the couch next to Cardell. "Waking the neighbors?"

"It's one in the afternoon," mumbled Cardell.

"Jesus," said Hicks, scratching his crotch. "What day?"

"Sunday."

"Shit," chuckled Hicks. "I missed church."

Hicks reached into his pocket and pulled out a crumpled napkin.

"I forgot about this," he said, his voice scratchy.

"What's it?"

"Jamie's number," said Hicks.

"Who's Jamie?"

"She's that riot girl from Craig's last night. The one in the purple pants."

"Oh right," said Cardell, still strumming on the guitar, cocking his head to the side. "She was hot."

"Yeah," said Hicks. "She was cool. I'll call her next weekend."

"Yeah, definitely."

"What's that you're playing?" asked Hicks, putting the napkin back in his pocket and motioning in the direction of the guitar.

"I don't know," replied Cardell. "Some tune I was dreaming this morning."

"Dreaming?"

"Yeah," said Cardell. "I dreamt I was playing this song on my guitar."

"Kind of like Keith Richards?"

"I s'pose."

"You should lay that down on the four-track," said Hicks.

Hicks grunted and rose from the couch. He went to a folding chair standing in the opposite corner of the living room and sat down. He bent over a blue

Tascam four-track recorder that was set up on a table made from a plywood sheet and four cinder blocks.

Hicks put on a set of over-ear headphones that were plugged into the four-track. Then he picked up a metallic Shure vocal mic, plugged into track one of the four-track, and placed the mic on the couch next to Cardell's guitar.

"Angle the guitar toward the mic," ordered Hicks, and Cardell adjusted his posture accordingly.

Hicks went back to the four-track recorder, sitting down on the folding chair, leaning over the makeshift table. He checked the levels on track one. Satisfied, he picked up a smoky glass pipe, the bowl glazed with black tar. He searched his jeans pocket and pulled out a baggy. He proceeded to stuff weed into the pipe.

Gene, a skinny Jewish kid as pale as Hades, sat up on the cot and stretched his arms.

"What time is it?" he asked.

"A little after one," said Hicks, toking on the bowl. "You can sleep in the bedroom if you want."

Gene stood up and dragged a sheet with him out of the room.

They met Gene at the youth hostel the day Robert left. They dropped Robert off at Port Authority. They watched him carry his duffel bag into the station. Then they drove off to find a parking garage. They used their last dollars on the parking fee and two beds in the youth hostel.

It was there in the smoking room they met Gene. Gene was wearing nothing but tighty-whities and a towel. His clothes had been stolen from the laundromat. They shared clothes and cigarettes with Gene.

Gene said he had signed a lease on a one-bedroom apartment, but he needed roommates to split rent. Cardell and Hicks jumped on board. They sold their van for scrap at the junkyard and paid for the apartment deposit. Five days later they were Brooklyn residents.

When Cardell finished laying down his guitar track, he gently returned the guitar to its case. Then he smoked another bowl with Hicks.

"You wanna see something cool?" asked Cardell. A vintage iron radiator, painted white, no longer attached to the steam valve, sat underneath the window where the box fan continued to blow. Cardell took the microphone over to the radiator and set it on top, the cord dangling behind.

"Put on the headphones," he said, waiting for Hicks to comply. Once he did, Cardell picked up a loose drumstick from the floor and began to rattle the radiator with it.

"That's way cool," said Hicks, with a big ol' grin. "But how are we going to play that in a show?"

"We'll figure something out," Cardell laughed. He put down the drumstick and removed the microphone from the radiator. Hicks took off the headphones.

"I need food," said Hicks.

"Ann's?" asked Cardell.

"That's what I was thinkin'."

"Let's finish this song first," said Cardell. "And smoke another bowl."

"Cool."

By the time they got to Ann's, a greasy diner on the main drag tucked between a consignment store and a payday loan joint, the school buses were driving by taking kids home from school. At Ann's, Cardell and Hicks devoured a plate of the three-ninety-nine all-day breakfast special.

"We should page Dex," said Cardell, dipping his toast into the runny yolk of his over easy eggs.

"The phone is disconnected," said Hicks, shoveling in a mouthful of greasy home fries. A smudge of mucky yellow yolk splotched his chin.

"We could get a phone card," said Cardell, taking a big gulp of coffee loaded with cream and sugar.

"Where would he call?" asked Hicks.

"We use a pay phone," explained Cardell. "We dial the pay phone number, followed by zero-five."

"What does that mean?"

"Fifty backwards," said Cardell. "It means we want a fifty sack."

"How do you know?"

"Dex told me last night at the after-party."

"Right on," said Hicks, mopping up the remains of his plate with his last bit of toast. "Hey, let's roll over to the park. There's a pay phone there. We can hack."

"Yeah man," said Cardell. "It's coolin' down. It's nice as hell outside."

***

Dex buzzed their apartment at seven-thirty. Cardell let him in.

"What's up fellas?" asked Dex. He was a skinny Black teenager with thick-lensed turtle glasses. His hair was braided back in cornrows. His Adidas T-shirt hung down to his knees, and he carried a navy-blue Timberland backpack. Gene crept out of the bedroom to join the guys in the living room.

"Dex, this is Gene," said Cardell. "Gene, this is Dex."

Cardell realized these were the only two people he knew in New York City.

"What's up?"

"What's up?"

"Cop a squat," said Cardell, sitting in the folding chair.

"I can only stay for a minute," said Dex, setting his backpack down on the couch. "I gotta meet my boy at Tower at eight."

"Fifty, right?" said Hicks, pulling a crinkled envelope from his backpack.

"Yeah," said Dex. "Hey, what are you guys up to? You should troop out wit' me."

Dex dug into his backpack and laid out a row of thick baggies on the dusty floor.

"Pick one for yourself," he said.

Cardell opened the thickest bag and took a deep whiff.

"That's skunky," he said with a smile.

"Fuck yeah," said Dex. "And it's not too stringy. Check out those fluffy buds."

Hicks examined the bag after Cardell.

"Fuckin' sweet," he said. Hicks handed Dex a wad of greenbacks from the envelope.

"All right, that wraps up the business portion of the evening," said Dex, as he packed away his product. He sorted through his backpack and pulled out a skinny sack of weed. "It's time for a little pleasure. Have you heard of Orange Crush?"

"No," said Cardell.

"It's some mad shit," said Dex with a big grin. "My boy got some Purple Crush, which is ridiculously dank, but was, you know, eighty for a G."

"Wow," said Hicks. "That must be dank."

"No joke," said Dex. He loaded the Orange Crush, which lived up to its name with its fuzzy orange hairs, into a small, glass pipe. Silver snakes slithered along the side of the bowl. Dex flicked a lighter and sparked the bud. Mary Jane's pheromones poured from the pipe and engulfed the room. Dex held the pipe out to Hicks. "Here, try some."

Hicks took a deep hit. His eyes bulged. He coughed. Smoke billowed out from his nostrils.

"Damn," he said, choking.

"I told ya, no joke," said Dex, chuckling. "Next time we roll us a mad blunt. None of this pipe shit."

Cardell took a big hit from the little pipe and passed it to Gene. Gene took the bowl, but it was cashed. Dex took the pipe from him and emptied the ash into an ashtray on the plywood table. He stood up straight and saddled on his backpack.

"I gotta roll," he said. "Why don't you guys come?"

"Where you goin'?" asked Cardell, his eyes glazed and bloodshot, a devilish smirk pasted across his face.

"I gotta get to Tower first, then one more delivery," said Dex. "Then I wanna check out the mixers at Daddy's."

"Sounds cool," said Hicks. "Lemme get my shoes."

"Me too," said Cardell, struggling to stand from the couch. "You comin', Gene?"

"Nah," said Gene. "I gotta do laundry. Work tomorrow."

"All right, we'll catch ya later," said Cardell. "You need a key?"

"Yeah, could you leave me one?"

"No problem."

Cardell, Hicks, and Dex took the stairs down three flights of stairs, the rickety wood creaking under each step. They floated out onto the street. The sun still hung over the New York skyline, but it was steadily making its descent. They lived on a narrow side street lined with slender apartment buildings covered in fire escapes. A squat Caribbean hooker waited down on the corner.

To get to Tower they passed along Prospect Park. Tank-topped girls and guys in oversized FUBU shirts streamed by, along with the occasional suit or hawker.

When they reached the record shop, Dex stepped up on the lamppost and waved to a dreadlocked dude wearing baggy jeans and a Yankees jersey.

"Hey Troy!" Dex hollered. "Over here!"

Troy sauntered over and slapped hands with Dex.

"What's up?" said Troy.

"Business as usual," said Dex. He turned to Cardell and Hicks who were trailing behind. "This is my boy, Troy. He mixes for me, lays down beats."

Then Dex turned back to Troy.

"This is Cardell and Hicks," said Dex. "They're a couple a rocks stars from Iowa."

"Iowa," said Troy with a bewildered guffaw. "What the hells you doin' in Brooklyn?"

"Just hangin' out," said Cardell, who towered over all of them. "Tryin' to be rock stars."

"Yeah?" said Troy. "Aren't we all."

"We gotta get over to Fifth," said Dex. He hustled them down the street and turned on Fifth Street. They shuffled to a brick apartment building with a manicured hedgerow. Dex rang the buzzer, and the front door buzzed open. They entered the building and went to an apartment at the end of the hallway. Dex knocked and a scruffy hippie answered. A skunky odor drifted into the hallway.

"What's up, Dex," said the hippy, wearing a tie-dyed Phish T-shirt and hemp necklace. "I was wondering if you'd show."

"Sorry, Doug," said Dex. "Got hung up with the boys."

Doug the hippie, who was even shorter than Hicks, opened the door wide and Dex eased into the apartment followed by Cardell and Hicks. Doug shook each of their hands as they entered. Troy came in last and wrapped his hand with a sheet of paper before shaking Doug's hand. They piled into a room filled with gleaming guitars and recording devices.

"Nice studio," Cardell marveled quietly.

"You guys play?" asked Doug, sitting down on a crocheted bean bag chair. "I'm selling some of my guitars."

"How much?" Cardell inquired.

"I'm sellin' this '69 Les Paul for five grand," said Doug, leaning over and grabbing the neck of a gold-bodied electric guitar.

"They're nice guitars, huh?" mumbled Cardell. "That's a little too much for me."

"How about you?" the weird little man asked Hicks.

"Got any basses?" asked Hicks, gruffly.

"I got one, but I'm not selling it," said Doug, strumming on the silent strings of the Les Paul. He gave a questioning look to Troy, who was leaning in the doorway.

"I play skins," Troy grumbled.

Dex pushed aside empty fast-food wrappers and set his backpack on a dusty mahogany coffee table in the center of the room.

"I got the Crush," said Dex, unzipping the backpack.

"How much?" asked Doug.

"Um, hundy," said Dex.

"Can I get it for sixty?"

"You still owe me a Benjamin," growled Dex.

"C'mon," whined Doug. "You know I'm good for it."

"How 'bout you pay me one-eighty or I bash that guitar over your head."

Cardell realized Troy had entered the room, and somehow the four of them had formed a posse in front of Doug the hippie. Doug's face went white.

"Okay, okay," mumbled Doug. "Just a sec."

He quickly returned the guitar to its stand, glancing at Dex to see if he was going to make good on his threat. Doug picked up backpack from the floor and rifled through it. He pulled out a wallet and shuffled through the bills.

"I got, I got sixty," said Doug.

"Okay," sighed Dex. "Gimme the sixty."

Doug handed over the sweaty bills. Dex passed over a thin baggy of Orange Crush.

"Next time," growled Dex. "You have my hundred or I'm taking your guitar."

"Yeah, yeah," said Doug with a sheepish grin. "Thanks, Dex. Really, thanks. I'll have your money."

With the transaction complete the barbershop quartet left Doug's apartment and roamed the twilight streets of Brooklyn.

"I can't stand that guy," muttered Troy, shivering on the street. "Look, I'm an opinionated motherfucker, but that guy is gross."

"Yeah," said Hicks. "His place's disgusting."

"Rich homeboy can't clean after himself," grumbled Troy.

"He had some pretty nice guitars and shit," said Cardell, lighting a cigarette.

"He does," nodded Troy, his dreads bouncing with the shake of his head. "He's one a those rich pricks that never learned to care a his things."

"True, true," said Hicks, lighting a cigarette of his own. "I grew up with nothing. So when I did get something, I took care of it. Once it's broke, it's gone."

"Exactly," said Troy.

"And it's the rich pricks that fuck you over," grumbled Hicks. "That god-damned Ben Schroeder. Took my distortion pedal, broke it, and played like nothin' happened."

"Where's the love anymore?" asked Troy. "Can't trust no one."

"Friendship is a fickle thing," said Dex. "We all have our reasons, to be friends, most of it is selfish. We have friends to make ourselves feel better. To feed that human beast inside of us. For most people back there in Nazareth, Jesus was just another dirty hippie."

"The F-man himself," Cardell muttered.

"Who?" asked Dex.

"Nothing," said Cardell. "Just something I remembered."

35

ONE SHINING STAR

August 30, 1996

There was that queasy feeling again. My abs knotted up, my throat constricted, my nostrils clogged with dry snot. It was a sensation that rolled through my body more and more often ever since Grandpa drove me back to Crawford Falls ten days ago.

I tipped my battered cap low over my eyes. There we were, a mob of kids, wandering up the sidewalk, hazily herding into the bars. Business was business, though. Jimenez had to keep his customers happy. He was definitely keeping me happy.

The line outside of Slim's was only ten people deep. The tinted picture windows flashed blues and yellows and pinks from within. The window vibrated from the bassline of the dance song bumping inside. (Thump-thump-thump.) The front door was propped open and the music melded with the muggy end-of-summer air. I craned my neck back, taking in the sky, the same sky that was always there no matter where you are.

This was the only section of Crawford Falls where you couldn't see the stars. The lights of the bars lining College Street obscured the night sky. When you get out in the residential area, or the parks, or even the cemeteries... or the golf course where you sneak onto the sixth green to lay out on a blanket with a bottle of wine, drop a tab, and just stare straight up, watching those specks of pyrite twinkle 'til dawn.

Standing in line with me were Western U college dudes with their backwards caps who stayed in town for the summer cleaning out the dorms and pounding Jäger bombs 'til bar close. I looked down at my feet. My toes peeked out of the leather straps of my sandals.

The big toe on my left foot had a light-pink scar. I don't remember how I got cut. I did remember waking up in the VW van that second morning out there in the New Jersey rest area. My toes had been caked in dried brown blood. When I washed it off in the gas station bathroom later, I saw it was barely a scratch. It's always those smallest scratches that bleed the most.

Jimenez and I were standing at the bar entrance now. I could smell the sweat and cigarette smoke and stale beer. We shuffled our feet through the door, hands in our pockets, trying not to bump into the girl and the guy walking in front of us. They were chatting.

"...and then I said, 'Statistically, God doesn't exist...'" the guy said.

This jackass must have taken beginning philosophy. He was wearing baggy slacks straight off the thrift shop rack and a silk, purple polo. His hair was frosted at the tips and spiked perfectly. And the girl. She wasn't bad looking, but she was laughing at his spiel. I felt bad for her. She could've been out with any other guy that night, but it just happened that this jerk was the one who asked first.

They were probably on the same dorm cleaning crew.

I caught her glimpsing at me out of the corner of her eye. Then her sparkling green eyes darted to Jimenez. Her eyes went dull. A frown of disgust almost engulfed her round face. Jimenez kept smiling his anarchist smile. He seemed to have that effect on most girls. Especially in this saltine cracker town.

It didn't help that he smelled like he just finished a ten-hour shift sweating over a fryer at the shrimp shack. Which he just had, and the stench poured from his body. He'd been wearing the same fatigue cut-offs the entire summer, as well as his periwinkle blue Helmet T-shirt that squeezed his rotund belly.

"Hey man let's go to Backbone tomorrow," Jimenez was saying to me.

"Where zat?" I asked.

"Out east, man," said Jimenez. "It's awesome."

"A'right," I said.

The couple in front of us paid their cover to the security guy sitting at the door and were swallowed up by the sea of gyrating bodies. I hope they get married and lose their house in an insurance scam.

"What's up, Pedro?" asked Jimenez in his nasally voice. The security guy, Pedro, and Jimenez slapped hands.

"Shit dude, just having a gay ol' time," snickered Pedro.

"Yeah, yeah, yeah," slurred Jimenez. "How's the party inside?"

"Same ol' shit," said Pedro, with a seedy, horny gleam in his eye. "You come on any good stuff lately?"

"As a matter of fact...," said Jimenez in a hushed voice, stooping down to talk in Pedro's ear. "Me and Rob are rolling pretty hard on some mad goodies right now."

Pedro chuckled. Jimenez stood up straight and slapped me on the shoulder.

"Aren't we Rob," he said with a big ol' shit-eating grin.

"Yeah, dude," I mumbled.

The doorman sized me up solemnly and swiveled back to Jimenez.

"I'll have to get a hold of you then," Pedro said to Jimenez.

"You got my pager number?"

"Yeah, somewhere."

"Give me a buzz then. Eight-oh-eight."

"Will do."

"Any fine honeys here tonight?" asked Jimenez, swaying into the bar, bobbing his head side to side like a peacock.

"Always," called out Pedro as we weaved our way into the sweaty crowd. Disco lights were flashing across the dance floor where pockets of college kids were grinding on each other.

Pedro was already collecting money from the next people in line as we began our mingle. Heads turned to check out the giant, dirty townie and his skinny white friend. It was a young crowd as usual. Sophomores and juniors learning what it's like to get plastered and hump. Out-of-town dirtballs in their FUBU wear and bleach-blonde hoes in miniskirts drooling in for a night in the city. Cubs hats and white, flabby thighs. Tongues probing, hands groping, and hormones pumping.

Shining like the stars. Pouring alcohol down their throats until they get laid or get in a fight. Girls, all a twitter, disingenuously trying to stop the fights. Then nature does it thing. Instinct. Survival of the fittest. Just because we, as human beings, wear clothes doesn't mean that we are excluded from the natural order of things.

In five years, these kids will either be squirting on themselves from behind a computer or digging up ditches to lay down more fiber-optic cables. Deep down they know this. Tonight, they are beasts.

I found myself in front of the bar polished with a sticky film of spilled beer and vodka. A blonde squeeze-queen was leaning against the bar, her head tilted back so her promulgated bosom ballooned out of her black halter top. Her glittering eyes inspected me, this starry-eyed ginger in a grass-stained undershirt.

A voice called out to me.

"Longley!"

I jerked out of my haze to find Pete looming from behind the bar. His cheery face beamed.

"Pete!" I called back in a gargling slur. I leaned on my elbows on the edge of the bar, sliding my sandal up onto the foot-rail. "What's going on?"

"Just working, man," he hollered, pouring a sudsy beer into a pint cup. He had curly unkempt hair and deep dimples that made the young girls squeal.

"What are you doing?" Pete hollered. "I thought you were in New York with Cardell and Hicks!"

"Yeah, I was," I mumbled sullenly. I glanced at the siren next to me. She was sulking that I was able to get the bartender's attention. "Got back like ten days ago."

"Why's that?" Pete shouted, pouring a waterfall of suds into the drain.

"Uhh," I stuttered, and then I chuckled, trying to relieve the pain gurgling in my stomach. "I pussed out, dude. I couldn't hack it in the big city."

"Uh huh," said Pete, nodding absently as he poured more beer into the foamy pint. "Where are Starsky and Hutch at?"

"They're still in NYC," I said, sliding a Marlboro Light out of the pack in my pocket and lighting it up. "Can I get a drink?"

"Sure, dude. What do you want?"

"Jack on the rocks."

"No problem."

I turned my back to the bar and took a drag off the cigarette. My stomach curdled. The varnished floor sloped down before me. Wait a minute, there's no barrier at the bottom. There are no brakes. Just as there really aren't any stars in the sky. The disco lights pulsated and throbbed.

Then I saw Virginia. She flashed by in a leopard mini-skirt and white blouse ruffled at the shoulders. She had put on the freshman fifteen since I last saw her. If she saw me, she didn't show it. The dropout has no clothes.

I checked to make sure my fly wasn't down.

"Here you go, Rob," Pete hollered from over my shoulder. I swiveled around to find a glass of honey setting before me.

"Thanks, Pete."

I sipped at the chilled goblet. My tongue was glowing. So was Pete.

"How much?" I asked.

"Don't worry about it."

"Thanks."

I scanned the Dionysian orgy writhing on the dance floor.

"I'm going to find Jimmy," I mumbled to no one in particular. Maybe it was to the pouting blonde standing next to me. I could feel an anxious warmth emanating from her. Best to leave her alone.

I hoisted my anchor from the bar and stumbled out into the crowd. I squirmed through, crotches and buttocks smushed into mine. Sweat rimmed around my brow. I found Jimenez at the other side of the dance floor in a softly illuminated hovel where two pool tables sat side-by-side. Jimenez was chatting in the corner with Schroeder, a candy kid from Omaha. His dad was a professor or something.

The legs of Schroeder's orange phat pants hooped around his ankles. A string of neon beads hung from his folded neck. Jimenez had his usual smug smile. His lips were inches from Schroeder's ear, which had a giant hoop in the lobe like an African tribeswoman.

Schroeder's eyes were glued to the balls skidding across the velvet felt of the pool table. As I veered in closer, I caught the tail end of Jimenez's last sentence. His voice was low, and sharp as a knife.

"...or I'm going to fucking break your legs off."

I planted my feet next to Jimenez, sipping at my Scotch.

"What' up, Jimmy?" I asked, keeping my eyes innocent, while also straightening my shoulders, crossing my arms to give my biceps a bulge.

"Hey, Rob," said Jimenez, turning from Schroeder, who had splotches of red sprouting up his pasty face. A puddle of sweat had soaked into the pits of his black, silk shirt. "Just chillin'."

Schroeder took the opportunity to slither away. Jimenez had a flat pint of beer in his hand. He suddenly squinted. His black eyes delved deep into mine.

"How you feeling?" he asked.

"I think I'm peaking," I said. My voice hovered in front of my face.

A thin brunette in Capri slacks flitted by. Whiskers grew out of her cheeks.

"That isn't the peak yet!" shouted Jimenez, with a guffaw. "Just wait!"

His cherubic cheeks morphed into craters as he laughed.

Suddenly a pool cue sliced through the air. I could feel the wind in its wake. There was a dull smack. A crack. Jimenez slumped into me, his meaty paws clutching at my shoulder. Schroeder screamed as he took another crack at Jimenez's back. This time the pool cue splintered in half. Jimenez swung his arm out, knocking the stick out of Schroeder's hands.

Three grisly demons glared from behind Schroeder. Their chests were plumed out. Schroeder had rounded up a posse.

Jimenez's hat had fallen off. His black mane straggled down his back. His shoulders heaved. With one mitt, he wrenched Schroeder by the collar. He smashed his right fist into Schroeder's fat face. Schroeder's nose burst. His knees buckled. He crumpled to the floor, cradling his gushing nose.

The three hoods pounced on Jimenez. I saw blazing eyes, gnashing teeth, and swinging fists. I grabbed onto one flailing arm. It tried to tear from my grip. My nails dug into his skin. I pried him off Jimenez. The demon stumbled into the gathering crowd. The onlookers tossed him back into the fray.

The unshaven face of another demon emerged from the shadows. My fingers ached as I curled them into my palm. With my weight on my right foot, my elbow cocked, I rammed my fist into his eye socket. I could feel his skull on my knuckles.

Momentum carried me over. I tumbled on top of him. We were tangled on the damp, grimy floor.

Two hands hauled me up from the ground. My foe was still down, curled up, clutching his face. Jimenez was being held by two security guards. His arms were taut, nostrils seething.

Pedro helped me to my feet.

"You guys better get out of here," he said, hoarsely. I nodded meekly. The demons were regrouping, holding their chins and glaring at us with hellfire.

"Yeah," I chuckled. "Let's go."

Pedro grabbed my elbow and led me to the door. There was a scuffle behind me as the two security guards dragged Jimenez behind us.

"Fuck you, you twats!" he was bellowing, a tiger roaring from its cage.

We paraded through a cloud. We made it to the door. We were shoved outside. The door slammed behind us.

The air outside chilled my bones. The midnight breeze brushed us into the empty street. Jimenez burst into hysterics. He bent over and screamed bloody murder at the pavement. I choked. Then I barked out a laugh.

"Fuuuuck!" I chuckled. "Good to be back in Iowa."

The hushed yellow glow of the streetlights swirled around my head. I stood still and craned my neck back, once again searching the sky.

The North Star beamed down at me through the haze.

36

A Minor

Inside the den with Mr. Longley

August 30, 1996

I do love my TV. Sony surround sound, forty-eight-inch screen, crystal clear reception, and 172 channels of digital satellite entertainment. And my leather recliner. Patent, soft, straight from the cow. Worn down to fit my jolly old ass. And nobody here to bother me. No kids fighting over the remote control. I can watch Baywatch in peace and quiet. Just me and Pamela Lee. Kristy's already in bed. Just better hope she doesn't come out for a drink of water.

Speaking of drink, my beer is almost empty. Miller Genuine Draft. That takes me back to my younger days. Pouring concrete for Paul. Three years of sand and water and dirt and sweat and Camel wides and MGD. Supporting a beautiful, young bride and a round, rooster of a toddlin' boy. Scraping by month to month. Rent for the trailer, phone bills, doctor bills, Robert's therapy, electric bills, car payments, student loans, credit cards, groceries, diapers, and with whatever was left over, beer. Somehow there was always money for beer and cigarettes.

Now I have enough money to buy a big screen TV, leather La-Z-Boy, a 2,500 square-foot house with a two-car garage filled with a Ford F-150, Honda Accord, and a 1997 Triumph Thunderbird, burgundy. I can send my kids to any college in the nation—if they had enough gumption to go.

Robert's been home almost two weeks... I'm glad he's home... He's my son... I wish... I wish I could let him live his life.

If only the boy would get off his duff. He just needs to fill out a registration form. He could go to any school he wants, with his brain. Damn kid got too smart for his own good. It's his decision, though. Dad forced me into college. I hated every day of it. Spent my days sleeping instead of going to class. Spent my nights at Casey's playing pool and shooting tequila poppers with Huggy Bear, sneaking out to the parking lot to smoke a joint. Man, that was fun. Can't do that anymore. I know Rob's out there doing the same damn thing. At least I don't have to pay for his Fs like my old man had to pay for mine. Lord, did he get pizzed after he saw my report cards. My stomach still churns. Robert will figure it out when he's ready. Or he will just have to learn the hard way, which took me ten years.

Run Pamela, run.

We let Robert back in with his tail between his legs. The least we can do is give him a roof over his head, so long as he pays the price. Rent is due tomorrow. That's one step toward adulthood. He needs to take the next step. On his own.

It's just those friends of his. Losers. Potheads. Dregs of society. At least he left those two idiots in New York. I hate to think what gutter they're sleeping in tonight. Rock 'n' roll stars my ass. I can show them a thing or two about rock 'n' roll. Clapton was God. Him, Ginger, and Jack, man. They jammed the gospel. It was like heaven was flowing through those chops and grooves. These bands today that Robert and his friends listen to... they're like a bunch of retards that were just released from their cages.

Robert's a decent drummer. Good thing Kristy forced him to take piano lessons for so many years. His friend Cody was a pretty good guitarist. I wonder why he never jams with him anymore. Good kid. Good family. It's just the way kids that age cycle through friends. Robert always had that drive in him to be part of the cool crowd. What a bunch of jerks. Robert's a good kid. Always does what he's told, works hard, goes out of his way to help others. An Eagle Scout.

So why does he have to hang out with these assholes that are lazy, cuss, drink, smoke dope. I know why they like Robert. He's naive, gullible. A people-pleaser. He just gives and gives, just so that he can hang out with fuckups. And they take advantage of him for all he's worth. I just hope that Robert's kindness rubs off on them a little. Well, for whatever reason, it's easier to be bad than good.

That's life. That's the way of the world. No matter how much you sugar coat it the bad guys are still running the show. They make the rules, they break the rules, but you better follow them to a T, or they will eat you alive, burn you at the stake, nail you to a cross.

All you can do is deal with it the best you can. I've served my purpose on this planet. I'm not going to change anything, but I kept my bloodline going. I planted my seed. I raised two healthy, intelligent children who will hopefully give back to the world. Robert just better not keep heading in the direction he is going.

Am I a good father? Did I fuck up somewhere? When Robert entered his teen years, we had our blowups. I wish I had handled them better. As a parent, you can always do better. But at least then I understood where he was coming from. He was trying out new personalities, new attitudes. He was just a kid trying on a new pair of jeans.

It just meant he felt safe with us. He felt safe trying out his new identity with his parents. I did my best to be patient and let him express his feelings, no matter how irrational. Just sometimes you're too tired to react rationally. Sometimes being a parent is an out-of-body experience. It's like you're watching yourself from above. You know you shouldn't shout. But you do, and you listen to the words coming out of your mouth, knowing full well that is the wrong thing to say. Spewing gasoline onto a testosterone fire.

At least Robert had the spark then. Sometimes it combusted, sure. Most of the time though, we could nurture his flame.

These days, the way Robert is acting lately, something's off. He's lost a light inside. If it doesn't spark again, he might not ever become a successful participant in society. He might never reach his potential. Staying out late, sometimes not coming home at all, working a dead-end job that barely pays over minimum wage, unshaven, unkempt. He needs a goddamn haircut. Hell, he lipped off to Kristy. I could've slapped him if I was there. She's worried to death about him. "He'll be all right, Kristy," is all I can say. She thinks he's on drugs. I know he's on drugs. I hope I'm doing the right thing.

It's almost two now. I wonder if he's coming home tonight. He better, he's driving the Honda. Speaking of the devil. There's the garage opener.

***

Goodnight 5-11-99 This One is for My Homies

Everything you wish you had never said

Every flower you regret not plucking

Every time that you just kept on sucking.

Get out of town.

Run for the hills.

Spray the screens down

and clean the windowsills.

Break your neck.

Take the check.

You think the sky is blue.

You think that you just might chew

on the bait.

They can wait.

Ain't no hurry.

Ain't so furry

with the gangrene baby heart.

Who's looking for the rock star?

Who needs the rock star?

What more can you ask for?

37

WHO DRINKS THE TEA FOR ITS TASTE?

September 3, 1996

"Think man, think!" Robert grumbled to himself.

He was lounging in a rocking chair on his parents' back porch. The seat of the chair was padded with a hard, leather cushion. Two dark buttock imprints had been worn in from years of use. Robert's father had claimed the sturdy chair after his grandfather had passed away at the ripe old age of 92. A transplant from the old family farm. Robert's red notebook stared blankly at him from his lap. The black pen he was gnawing on protruded from his lips.

He squinted into the sun for some sort of revelation. All he received were red splotches flashing in his corneas. He peered into the fir trees that surrounded the backyard and saw a couple of sparrows fluttering among the branches.

The air was cooler. Fall was approaching. The start of a new school year. For the second time, Robert wasn't going. Last year, he was filled with excitement for the unknown. This year was blasé, like watching summer reruns.

Robert turned at the sound of the screen door sliding open behind him. His sister, Jessica, bopped out onto the porch, her shiny, silky hair pulled back into a ponytail. She was wearing a baby-blue tank top and a pair of Daisy Dukes, leaving much of her scrawny body exposed to the September sun.

"What are you doing?" she asked, placing her feet on the curved planks of Robert's rocking chair so it tilted back. Robert gripped the armrests.

"Nothing," he said. He closed his notebook and slipped his pen into the spiral.

"Are you writing about me?" Jessica asked, and she started to rock the chair.

"Yeah, I'm writing about the time Mom and Dad took us to see Santa and you told him that what you wanted for Christmas was a pair of 'big tits,'" Robert jeered, tilting his head back and giving his sister a big old grin.

"You wouldn't dare, you jerk," Jessica laughed, grabbing a lock of his red hair and yanking it.

"Ouch," said Robert, wrenching his head from his sister's clutches.

"I was only four!" Jessica giggled. "And you told me to say that! I didn't even know what it meant."

Jessica jumped from the chair and climbed onto the wooden fence bordering the porch, careful to avoid knocking over the potted aloe vera. Robert had helped his father build that fence.

"I thought it was pretty funny," said Robert, still grinning.

"Well, Mom and Dad didn't."

"Tell me about it."

"Yeah, well Dad's being an asshole again today," said Jessica with a pout. She pouted with the best of them.

"Watch your language," said Robert. "What's wrong?"

Robert shivered as he realized the sun had dipped behind the trees, blanketing the backyard in shadows.

"Dad won't let me go out tonight," said Jessica, perched on the fence, her hands tucked under her arms.

"Well, you shouldn't," said Robert. "It's a school night."

"But I don't have any homework, and it's not like I have any tests. I usually skip homeroom anyways," Jessica whined. "Besides, you got to go out on school nights all the time."

"And look where I am now," said Robert. "Anyway, I didn't start going out on school nights until I got my license. Then all me and my friends did was sit around and watch TV and play cards. What do you want to do tonight?"

"Oh my God! You will not believe it!" squealed Jessica. She hopped off the fence, waving her hands, contorting her face like Tweety Bird. "Jeff Bell asked me to go to a party at his house!"

"Oh yeah, I heard about that," said Robert. "Is he gonna have a keg?"

"I don't know. But he is so totally the coolest guy in school. And everybody is going to be there. I just have to go!" exclaimed Jessica, flailing her hands as she spoke.

"How are you going to get there?"

"Well, I was hoping you would give me and Steph a ride."

"I suppose you want me to talk to Dad, also?"

"Please?" pleaded Jessica, squeezing her hands together in prayer and batting her sparkling, blue eyes at Robert.

"I have to work tonight," he said.

"What time?"

"Eight to close."

"Well, the party doesn't start 'til nine," said Jessica, tapping her bottom lip. "I don't suppose you could drop us off at, like, Brynna's? She only lives, like, a block away from Jeff's."

"That is, if Dad lets you go."

"I still have a few more tricks up my sleeve."

"I'm sure you do. And how do you plan on getting home?"

"Um, what time do you get off work?"

"Around midnight."

"Um, could you pretty please..."

"Yeah, yeah. You're begging sickens me. I can drive you and your friends home. I just expect an extra big birthday present. You still owe me one."

"Oh, thank you! Thank you!" cried Jessica, throwing her arms around Robert's neck, making the rocking chair go haywire. "I'll buy you a new car!"

"It better be a convertible," Robert grumbled, shaking off his sister. Jessica let go of him and started for the door. Then she paused.

"Did you have a keg for your birthday?" she asked.

"Not this time."

"Did you go to any keggers in New York?"

"Yeah, we crashed a party in Manhattan."

"Really?"

"Yeah, it was pretty crazy."

"What happened?"

"I'll tell you when you're older."

"Oh, c'mon!" huffed Jessica. Robert just smirked.

Venus was now twinkling above the tips of the evergreens from whence the sun had finally given its curtain call. The iridescent glow of the last firefly of the season danced in the air, then disappeared as quickly as it came. Robert rose from the chair, tucked his notebook under his arm, and followed his sister into the house.

38

THERE IS ONLY ONE STORY TO BE TOLD

September 21, 1996

My grandpa sat down next to me on the couch in my Aunt Kristy's living room. I was too big to sit on his lap. We had returned from the church where they were preparing for my cousin Bobby's funeral. When we got back to my aunt's house, I wanted to play. It did not go well.

"We all make mistakes sometimes," my grandpa said. He smiled warmly, his wrinkles the wake of a lightning bolt.

I rubbed my reddened nose and sniffled and wiped my finger on my pant leg.

"I didn't mean to," I whimpered.

Grandpa laid his arm over my shoulders and tugged me to his side. I could smell his cool aftershave. His chest was warm and comforting. I could still hear my aunt sobbing in the kitchen.

"I know, I know," Grandpa said, soothingly. "Sometimes it's just best to leave things alone."

"I said I'm sorry," I said with another sniffle.

"Yes, and that was the right thing to do," said Grandpa, with a warm smile. "Let's go get you cleaned up for dinner."

He enveloped my tiny hand in his and led me to the bathroom.

"Do you know what the cow said to the moon?" Grandpa asked. He turned on the faucet in the bathroom. I shook my head, "No."

"Moove over, because I'm comin' up!" Grandpa exclaimed. I laughed sheepishly along with my grandpa's wheezing chuckle.

Grandpa washed my hands thoroughly and dried them in a hand towel. I followed him to the dinner table. Two leaves had been placed in the center of the table to extend it. It filled the whole dining room at my Aunt Kristy's house. The table was loaded down with bowls of various casseroles, vegetables, and breads.

I took the seat with the glass of milk. My chair knocked into the wall when I pulled it out. I winced, ready for another scolding. Nobody said anything and I sat down. I used to sit on a phone book when we had big family dinners. Now my chest reached the table top without any support.

Aunt Kristy, dressed in a black blouse, came into the dining room carrying a bowl of creamed corn between hot pads. Her cheeks were red and puffy. My mother glared at me as she set down the butter dish. Grandma brought in the roast chicken and placed it at the center of the table. She sat in the chair at the head of the table. Grandpa sat down across from her clear down at the other end.

The family filled out the rest of the chairs. My cousin Jessica, dressed in loose sweats, her face deathly pale, sat next to me. She gave me a weak smile and squeezed my hand.

"Shall we say grace?" asked Grandma.

We bowed our heads in reverence.

"Lord, bless us for this day," said Grandma. "And for all those that could be with us. We pray that you keep the sun shining bright, and the air pure and clean. Please bless this food before us, and bless those less fortunate than ourselves. And Father, bless our Bobby, who you decided to take from us. May his soul rest in heaven. Amen."

We all rang out in chorus, "Amen."

Earlier, my stomach was growling. Now it was clenched tight. From where I sat I could still see my Cousin Bobby's baseball mitt lying on the floor in the living room. I found it in his old bedroom and thought it would be fun to play with. Then my Aunt Kristy saw me throwing a ball in it, making the webbing smack.

Her face went slack. She started wailing.

I was too scared to move. All I could do was let the mitt drop off my hand and onto the floor. What else were you supposed to do with a baseball mitt?

39

PREACHER TALK AT THE BALL GAME

September 4, 1996

Robert toed the steps to find his footing as he ascended the staircase. Halfway up, a light clicked on upstairs in the kitchen. Robert was at the point of no return. He paused, then continued his climb, laboriously. The fuzzy image of his father, clad in his dark blue bathrobe, waited for him at the top.

"Sorry if I woke you," Robert mumbled as he reached the top step, keeping his eyes low.

"I couldn't sleep," growled his father.

Robert nudged past him and walked into the kitchen. He opened the fridge and peered inside. He stared, then closed it, empty-handed. He was having déjà vu. This was his modus operandi. Robert stumbled home in the wee hours of the night, or morning, and tried to find his bed in which to pass out. He could always feel the presence of his parents, rustling in their bed, alert for Robert's nocturnal prowling.

This night, however, his father decided to confront Robert.

"I worry about you," his father said from the kitchen doorway.

"You shouldn't."

"I can't help it."

They stared at each other in equal silence, Robert leaning on the kitchen counter.

"I know what you and your friends are up to," his father said. "I'm not stupid. I thought I could let you live your life, but I can't do it anymore."

"I don't know what you're talking about," Robert slurred.

"Don't lie, it's not your nature," his father spat. "You reek of booze and smoke."

Robert's stench had permeated the sterile kitchen.

"I'm sorry," Robert offered.

"What you do to yourself is none of my business. You're nineteen now. Do whatever you want, nothing I say matters anyway. But what really pisses me off is that you drive your mother's car drunk. Do you have any clue what the consequences could be? I spent fifteen grand on that car. It's only half paid for. And that's just for the car. Throw in bail money, or worse, funeral expenses. Your jerky actions would not only put you in a world of hurt, but your mother and I will pay also. Pay big time."

"Nothing's gonna happen," said Robert. "I didn't drink that much."

"Sure, maybe you haven't. But there's other jackasses out there who have," growled his father. "And if a cop finds even just a whiff of beer on your breath, he will haul you in."

"I know."

"Do you? Then why do you do it?" Robert's father was almost shouting. "I didn't raise you to be an idiot. Sometimes I wonder if I did something wrong. And sometimes I wonder if I should have even tried. I have loved you like my own son, haven't I?"

"Yes," said Robert, leaning back against the counter, chin drooping against his chest. He couldn't have this conversation. Not in this state.

"That's another reason I worry," his father continued. "I lay awake thinking you're going to end up just like your father. That... we're going to find your mother's car smashed into a bridge pylon... and a note pinned to your flannel shirt."

"You don't need to worry..." Robert said, his quivering voice trailing off.

"Depression is hereditary, you know," said his father. "And you are so much like him, it terrifies me. Do you remember your dad?"

Robert shook his head.

"I guess you would have been too young," his father said quietly. "He was a good man. His head just wasn't attached. He was always writing poetry or writing songs or painting. We called him Leonardo. He was a big drinker, too. And he smoked a lot of dope and dabbled in some other stuff. He had a big heart, but his will was weak. I don't want you to turn out the same way. I love you, Robert. I want you to be a successful, productive member of society. I need you to be strong. I need you to be able to look me in the eye."

Robert kept his head low. His pupils quivered. His father tilted his head to try to catch Robert's eyes. It didn't work.

"Okay," Robert mumbled.

"I'm going to bed now," said his father. "I have work in the morning. Be around for dinner. I want to talk to you about going to school."

"Okay."

Robert stood alone in the kitchen, brooding over the pukish brown tile.

He woke up the next morning in his bed wearing the same clothes, only he was missing a sock.

40

Julie East Coast Productions

September 9, 1996

Robert lowered his shorts around his ankles and sat down on the cold, white porcelain seat in the basement bathroom of his parents' house. He checked to make sure there was enough toilet paper. The cotton roll was full. All was well in the world. Robert picked up his red notebook from the floor and he set it on his bare lap. He swiped his black pen out from the spirals and clicked off the cap. Robert set the tip of his sword to the paper and wrote:

***

Jessica stepped out of the car. Her mid-heeled shoes clicked on the concrete floor of the garage. She had bought the shoes, along with her dress, new for the funeral. Her father helped her mother out of the passenger side of the Ford F-150. Normally they would have drive the Accord, but…

It was smashed to pieces.

It was just the three of them in the garage. Jessica. Her mom and dad. It usually was just the three of them together. Now it felt like they were missing a limb.

Jessica's mother was still dabbing at her puffy, tear-streaked eyes. At least she wasn't heaving out sobs like she had been for the entire ride home. Jessica had just stared out the window in silence, doing her best to block out the noise, holding back her own tears.

She lost control of herself when she viewed Robert's body lying in the coffin. He was so stiff and still. Robert was never still. Even when he was sitting down, his fingers were always drumming out some cadence, or his feet were tapping some beat that only Robert knew.

Jessica had almost convinced herself breath was blowing out of Robert's nostrils. She so badly wanted him to wake up. Just wake up, end this, and come home.

Her father had to lead her away from the coffin. Jessica would never see her brother again.

The family of three entered the house. Jessica left her parents in the kitchen, where they stood, staring blankly at the island, at the large Tupperware caked in the remnants of their aunt's tuna casserole. They knew they should eat. They should feed Jessica. They should...

Jessica went straight to her bedroom. She dropped herself on her bed and slipped off her dress sandals. She grabbed her pink, laced pillow and clutched it to her stony breast. The bulletin board hanging above her desk was covered in polaroid pictures. A giant red heart cut out of construction paper surrounded the photo of her new boyfriend, Adam. Robert's senior picture was pinned right next to it. His cheeks were flushed, and he flashed that cracked, toothy, bashful grin.

A ferret started to claw from inside Jessica's stomach, making its way up, trying to burst out of her chest. Jessica darted her eyes away from the bulletin board and sat on the edge of her bed, gulping down her sobs.

She unzipped the back of her black dress and let the shoulder straps drape down. This was the only dress she ever hated shopping for. The dress slunk to the floor, and Jessica stepped to her closet. She peeled off her slip. Dropping it to the floor, she rummaged through her hangers.

Jessica left her room wearing an oversized Old Navy sweatshirt and pink tights. The light from her parents' bedroom shown from underneath the shut door. In the living room, her younger cousins' toys were scattered all over the floor. Robert's baseball mitt was still lying where her youngest cousin, Sammy, had dropped it.

Jessica picked it up and tugged it over her left hand. Kirby Puckett's scribbled autograph was engraved in the palm. Robert had received it as a Christmas present when he was a kid. He was elated when he received it. He kept it wrapped tight in rubber bands. He oiled it religiously. He sat in front of the TV, smacking a ball into the webbing over and over to loosen it up.

Jessica squeezed the glove shut a couple of times, then took it off, placing it on the side table of the couch.

A flash of light caught her eye. She walked to the bay window and peered out into the backyard. Her dad was sitting on the back porch alone. The dull red ember of his cigar seared as he puffed on it, staring at the sunset. Jessica watched him for a few seconds then turned away. She walked down the hall and stopped in front of the door to Robert's room.

She had not been in here in months it seemed. Robert never explicitly told Jessica to stay out of his room, but it was certainly implied. Since the accident, no one dared open the door. No one wanted to let Robert's last breaths escape. Now, the door was slightly ajar. Jessica tapped it open and tiptoed inside. The shadowed room had a cluttered neatness. Assorted papers were strewn atop his desk. His bedspread was crookedly draped over the bare mattress. A coil of rope snaked out of the closet.

Jessica lowered herself into the swivel chair at Robert's desk and flipped on his lamp. Robert had made the lamp out of a pop can in shop class. He was so proud of it, because it was the only thing he ever made that worked.

Books, magazines, and assorted notebooks wallowed on the shelves above his desktop. Jessica sniffed. She pulled open the top drawer of the desk. It rattled with lighters, matches, empty film canisters, and a toothbrush, still in its box.

Jessica gagged on a sob and closed the drawer. She wiped her eyes and jimmied open the second drawer. The red notebook that Robert always wrote in was lying on top of a stack of paper. She lifted out the notebook and shut the drawer. With trembling hands, Jessica leafed over the cardboard cover. She felt like a historian sifting through ancient texts.

On the first page, Robert had only written one single word: "IMMORTAL-ITY." A teardrop plunged from Jessica's eye duct and blotched the paper. She brushed her cheek. There was something scribbled on the inside of the cover.

Dear Mom and Dad,

When you find this notebook, I only ask you one thing. Please try to publish this book. That is my last wish.

Love,

Robert.

Jessica dropped the notebook to the desktop. She laid her head in her hands and cried with every bit of strength she had.

***

There was a light rapping on the door of the bathroom.

"Robert, Robert!" his mother called. "Are you all right in there?"

"Yeah, Mom. I'm fine!" Robert called back. He scribbled one more note in the notebook at the bottom of the last page: *This is the end.*

He set his notebook and pen on the tile floor and grabbed a wad of tissue.

"Well, you've been in there a long time," his mother called. "Come help with the dishes."

"Okay, just a second," said Robert.

He flushed the toilet and went to help his mother.

41

ONCE YOU THINK ABOUT IT

August 19, 1996

"So, do you have a girlfriend?" asked Reverend Brewer slyly. The silence in the car had gotten the best of him. Normally, he enjoyed the solitude of the open road. Good old peace and quiet. Time to reflect. Time to conjure his next sermon. But when he was with other people, an internal light switch flipped on and his gift of gab could not be contained.

"No," said Robert. He didn't relax his gaze from the window.

"Are you the type that has a wife in every port?" asked Reverend Brewer, offering a meek chortle with his joke. This did get Robert's attention.

"I thought I was. I mean, I wanted to be a.... a player," said Robert. "That's what being a rock star is all about."

"Sex, drugs, and rock 'n' roll," said Reverend Brewer, nodding, watching the highway ahead of him.

"Exactly," said Robert, turning his gaze to the windshield. "I had plenty of drugs. Plenty of rock. All I needed was the sex part."

"Did you find it?" asked Reverend Brewer gently.

Robert returned his gaze to the rolling countryside.

"Yeah," he said. "Once."

"And?"

"And what?"

"What happened?"

"I mean, there wasn't much to it. Just a one-night fling. Just... dirty, dirty... sex," said Robert with a hint of disgust in his voice. "Now I can't bring myself to look another girl in the eye. Like, all I see is sex in their eyes. This dirtiness. I can't give them what they want. It's not what I want."

"What is it that you want?"

Robert sighed.

"I really don't know anymore," he said.

"Have you ever been in love?" asked Reverend Brewer. "Sorry for being so bold."

"No that's alright," said Robert. There was silence again in the car except for the rattle of a pen setting atop the dashboard.

"Yes," said Robert, finally. "I was in love."

The words croaked out of Robert's mouth. Reverend Brewer let the silence continue.

"Everything made sense then," said Robert, once again filling the void. "My heart was hers. My soul was hers. My life was hers. She took it all. Now it means nothing to her. I was just her accessory. Something to look good on her arm. Then, when I became unfashionable, I was tossed aside. Tossed in the garbage."

"I'm sorry to hear that," said Reverend Brewer quietly.

"I guess... I mean... I thought I was over her," said Robert. "But I really just buried it under all of the shit I've poured into my body. Smothered it all in a pillow of fucking alcohol and weed. Excuse my language. But man, it's been a minute since I thought of that girl. She was hot, no lyin'. You should have seen us together. I thought it would be forever."

Robert shook his head and revealed a smirk. He continued.

"You could say, I suppose that she's the reason that I am where I am. Here with you, riding in this car, wherever it is we are. Lost in the traffic of America. Wandering like a toad in the rain. Searching for some long, lost answer, some sign that just makes sense out of everything. She's the reason I want to be a rock star. To show her exactly what I am. What I can become. What she's missing. What she threw away."

"So," said Reverend Brewer. "Why are you coming back? Is she... still around?"

"No, she's back in New York. Just a different part of New York. I was in the gutter. She's in the ivy," said Robert. "I don't know why I'm coming home. I guess because the answer isn't out there. I was running away from the answer without realizing it. It was right here all along. I was just too dumb to accept it."

"And so," said Reverend Brewer. "What's the answer?"

"I thought it was love," said Robert. "I thought it was rock 'n' roll. What else is there?"

"There's always God," said Reverend Brewer, glancing furtively at Robert.

A green road sign flashed in the low beams of Reverend Brewer's car. "Des Moines," it read.

"Here we are," said Reverend Brewer. "Where do you want me to drop you off?"

"You can leave me at the first gas station," said Robert. "I can call my grandpa from there."

"I can take you to his place," said Reverend Brewer.

"Well...," said Robert. "I don't know exactly where he lives. Honest, it's no problem. You've done enough.... Thanks, man."

Reverend Brewer pulled off at the next exit and pulled into an Amoco station. The blue, red, and white sign glowed bright as darkness took over the night.

"I can wait here to make sure you get a hold of him," said Reverend Brewer.

"No, seriously," said Robert. "You've helped me more than enough already. You have my deepest gratitude. I wish I had some money to help with gas."

The car was idling now in the parking space. Robert opened the passenger door.

"Gibberish," said Reverend Brewer. "The Lord works in mysterious ways. We were meant to meet each other."

"I'd like to think so," said Robert, looking back at Reverend Brewer, offering his hand. Reverend Brewer took it and gave Robert a firm handshake.

Reverend Brewer released and shifted his body, reaching into his back pocket. He pulled out his wallet. Robert started to wave him off.

"Here's my business card," said Reverend Brewer, pulling a white card out of this wallet, along with a greenback. "And here's five dollars, just to help you out."

Robert began to object.

"No, no. Just take it," admonished Reverend Brewer. "Stay on your path and the Lord shall give you your answer. If you are ever in Minneapolis, give me a call."

"I will," said Robert. "Thank you."

Robert shook Reverend Brewer's hand one more time. Then he stepped out of the car and shut the door. Robert watched Reverend Brewer back out of the parking space and gave him a wave. The car pulled back onto the Avenue of the Saints. Robert stood alone between the gas pumps, the blaring light of the Amoco sign glaring down on upon him.

42

Help! I'm in a Box

September 7, 1996

The speckles and the textures of the boulders of Backbone swam before Robert's eyes. The trees shimmered and the trout streams sang. The forest air cleansed Robert's lungs.

So, he lit a smoke.

He and Jimenez had spent their first day at Backbone exploring the limestone cliffs of the park's namesake—The Devil's Backbone hiking trail. Millions of years ago the land of Iowa was at the bottom of an ancient sea. The shells and sediment lying under the seabed were compressed by centuries of tremendous pressure, forming towers of limestone. When the temperature turned and the seas subsided and the loose dirt washed away, the limestone cliffs remained.

Now Robert and Jimenez were climbing all over these limestone cliffs like stoned ants in a jagged rock garden.

The drive from Crawford Falls to Backbone State Park had been a queasy exercise in déjà vu for Robert. He and Jimenez cruised down the interstate in Jimenez's 1982 shit-brown Datsun, this glorified matchbox car that he was always tinkering on in his garage. Jimenez and Robert passed bones back and forth as they rolled past waves and waves of cornfields, where the tan corn grew taller than a farmer's cowlick would soon be ready for harvest.

This land was once useless to the natives and the pioneers that subsequently pushed them out. Prairie grass taller than a covered wagon sprouted from the black soil like God's carpet. However, there weren't any trees with which to build cabins or even teepees. The nomadic Ioway tribesmen kept to the North Woods or followed the bison west. When the farmers arrived. They razed the tall grasses and planted cornfields.

Jimenez and Robert drove through a sea of corn smoking grass and blaring tunes.

"Soul Coughing?" asked Jimenez.

"No," said Robert. "Put in Clutch."

The route was the same route Robert, Cardell, and Hicks had taken to New York. Robert was relieved when they pulled off the interstate and followed the state highways and the local roads and finally the dirt roads to Backbone.

Robert thought when he returned to Crawford Falls he could turn over a new leaf. Restart fresh and clean. Instead his first night home he got in a fight with his dad and ended up at Jimmy's house. Jimmy's weed enterprise had diversified. In addition to baggies of marijuana he was selling an array of psychedelics and stimulants. Robert was his test audience. He'd find God another day, or in another way.

At Backbone, Robert and Jiminez set up their tents in the primitive campsites hidden in the back corner of the campground in the shade of the scraggly burr oak, far away from the prying eyes of the retirees set up at the electric sites with their RVs and pop-up campers, limp American flags hanging from flag poles attached to their bumpers.

Jimenez brought a sandwich bag filled with sugar cubes dosed with liquid LSD. Robert let the first one melt in his mouth while he staked in the corners of his green pup tent. He collected sticks in the woods and scared off some wild turkey. The acid kicked in when the fire was blazing.

Robert wasn't hungry, so he sat on a log and watched the flames lick at the air molecules.

They spent the first day exploring the limestone cliffs. Robert had brought along a length of parachute cord he intended to use for climbing, but once he got out the string he realized it was too skinny to hold any weight.

On the second day they went to the cave. At the car park Jimenez pulled out a fly rod and tackle box from the trunk of the Datsun. They stumbled over to one of the babbling trout brooks. Jimenez flipped the lure over the waters. They spotted trout wavering in the clear stream, but they refused to bite. Jimenez got his line tangled in the thistle and called it quits.

They followed a dirt trail through tall nettles that tore at Robert's jeans. One thorn caught the back of Robert's hand, and the poison stung like all get out. The dense forest gave way to limestone boulders and a rolling ridge as tall as St. Patrick's Church.

The cave was a dark hole halfway up the ridge. Robert and Jimenez climbed polished rocks up to the cave entrance.

As soon as they stepped under the rock awning of the cave entrance, the temperature cooled, like a walk-in fridge. The height of the cave quickly dwindled to the point where Robert and Jimenez had to hunch down. The rock floor was wet, slippery with a film of mud.

"Let's go in," said Jimenez.

"Um...," said Robert. "Okay."

Robert placed his hand on the wet wall and eased into the cave. The walls narrowed to shoulder-width, and they reached a cavern where they had to duck down low and squeeze in sideways. The buttons of Robert's flannel shirt knocked against the cave wall. The cavern within was pitch black. Robert began his descent and stopped. He backed out, nudging Jimenez's soft belly out of the way.

"What's wrong?" asked Jimenez, with a snide tone, sucking in to let Robert pass.

"It's too tight," said Robert. "Shit, I'm not goin' in there."

"Chicken," chuckled Jimenez. "Let me see."

Robert backed out into the safety of the cave entrance. He watched as Jimenez contorted his Play-Doh-like body to fit within the cavern corridor.

Jimenez disappeared. Robert could hear scraping and scuffling. Then Jimenez called out, "Cool beans, man!"

"Is it okay?" called out Robert.

"Yeah, man," called back Jimenez, his voice getting more muffled, receding deeper into the cave. "This shit is the tits. Get your ass in here."

Robert stared at the cavern entrance. He gave a slight shiver. The cave smelled of soggy worms. He didn't want to go any further. He wasn't going to go any further.

Jimenez was silent now. How far in did he go? Another shiver ran through Robert. What if Jimenez couldn't get out? What if he got stuck in there like Pooh Bear? They wouldn't let stoners just wander about inside the cave if it wasn't safe, would they?

"Everything okay?" called out Robert. Silence.

He stared at the dark hole that led deeper into more and more caverns carved out in the limestone bluff. How far did it go? The darkness enveloped Robert's vision. The molecules swirled in gray, like incense smoke caught in a draft.

A face emerged in the molecules. Round black eyes, sharp cheekbones, and a toothy, mealy grin. The mouth opened wide. Then the whole universe rushed at him. Stars and galaxies erupted from the cave. Robert could touch the nothingness of the void. He could feel the everything of the universe. He was looking at a mirror.

Nothing in one hand. Everything in the other. Clap them together. What do you get? It doesn't matter. In the end you get what you get. Nothing more, nothing less.

A voice appeared inside Robert's mind.

"Everything's going to be all right," it said, clear as crystal.

"The F-man," Robert mumbled.

The galactic face disappeared. The cave was an empty void. The emptiness filled Robert's heart.

Jimenez reappeared in the cavern entrance, squeezing his shoulders through the hole where the demon face had been.

"Cool shit," said Jimenez with a big grin. He stumbled out into the cave entrance. "You should check it out."

"No," Robert said. "I'm good. What was in the cave?"

"It was awesome, man," gushed Jimenez. "It was like... the inside of a centipede. Only, like, covered in bat shit."

They walked out into the cave clearing. Drops of rain were falling through the forest canopy.

"It's raining," said Jimenez.

"Yep," said Robert.

The rain kept up for the rest of the day. Jimenez and Robert cruised around the country roads smoking dope and listening to tunes until sunset. They picked up a load of dry firewood from a roadside stand. Back at their camp Robert set up the rain fly over the fire ring. He lit a fire underneath the tarp.

He stayed up all night tending the fire.

In the morning, the rain stopped, and they drove home.

43

IT ALL COMES TO THIS

September 9, 1996

Robert fingered the keys in his pocket.

Should I go? he thought.

He wavered outside the door of his mother's sleek Honda Accord. The garage was dark. Everything was dark. The dark silhouette of his father's Ford F-150 towered on the other side of the Honda. Robert glanced at the entry door leading into his parents' house. Stale, defeat. Thunder rumbled outside.

He had spent three days in the wilderness searching for a meaning. He was exhausted. It was time for Robert to go meet the F-man Himself.

Robert grabbed the keys from the pocket of his blue jeans and opened the car door. He slid into the driver's seat. He punched the sun visor and the garage door chachunged and groaned over his head.

Robert's mom and dad definitely heard that. They for sure knew he was taking the car out.

They'll ask me tomorrow where I went, Robert thought. *Do I tell them the truth? I guess nowhere is the truth. One of many, that is.*

He turned the key in the ignition and the engine turned over, purring just like Virginia did last night. It was another fucked up Sunday. Today was Monday. Most people don't like Mondays. They gotta go to school. They gotta go to work. Not Robert. Mondays were his days. His day of rest. His day of mourning.

Robert backed the car into the driveway, and out into the pouring rain, just like Agnes Falls up in the Boundary Waters where he showered after a day of canoeing on a camping trip with his friends. His old friends. He could feel the gallons of water dumping onto his head, a giant force of gravity, pounding at his body. But he climbed that fucking waterfall. Laboring every step. Clawing at cracks in the slippery rock face, his feet slipping in smoothness that only comes from centuries of wear. Straining every muscle. Little John, Cody, Keith, Mike, and Kiljoy, all cheering him on from below. Their voices barely reached his ears. The roar of the falls rushed over him.

The F-man was with him then. Directing every finger hold. Helping him feel out each crease in which he could plant his bare toes. Then he was at the top of the waterfall. Looking down, thirty feet, at his friends. The water tumbling towards them, crashing, smashing, infinite.

Now he was driving down his parents' street, the windshield wipers clearing the downpour from his vision.

Man, that Boundary Waters trip was ages ago, Robert thought. *How old was I? Thirteen? That was our first Boy Scout trip together.*

Robert turned down Highway 20 and headed east out of town. The headlights highlighted the rain spattering on the highway rushing ahead. He had the road to himself. Nobody else was out driving on a night like this. They'd have to be crazy.

Last night was fucking crazy. At least it was a nice day for it.

The first thing he did yesterday was roll over in his tent and take a swig out of a bottle of Johnny Walker Red. Sweet candy. Then he and Jimenez dropped another sugar cube and made the three-hour drive home from Backbone, taking breaks to smoke a J every now and then.

Now driving in his parents' Honda, Robert pulled a Clutch tape out of his back pocket and popped it in the car stereo. Good ol' Neil. Sing that song so sweetly.

Robert and Jimenez got back in town around eight last night and picked up Ogre. Then the three hoodlums showed up at Slim's. Robert never left the bar. Screaming Nazi, Rolling Rock chaser. Lemon drop. Jose Cuervo, Rolling Rock chaser. No stopping, no slowing down. Cigarette after cigarette.

Then Virginia plopped down on the stool next to him, snuggled up real cozy like, twitching that cooter under his nose.

Indeed, Robert thought. *Everything is gonna be all right.*

Virginia smelled just like cotton candy. Robert did some body shots off her well-endowed cleavage. She laughed and laughed. Robert slipped his hand down the back of her low-ride jeans and massaged her buttock. So fleshy, so ripe. She cuddled in even closer. Her plump breasts, poking at his elbow. Her breath cascading over his neck more seductively than Agnes Falls. Her lips tickling his ear.

Next, they were at her apartment. Robert, jamming his tongue down her throat. Her hand, groping at his gorged cock. Then his hands, kneading those two heaving tits. His mouth suckling at her soft, brown nipples. Then he was on the bed. He watched her, standing before him, tugging her tight jeans down to her ankles. Her vivacious body glowing in the flickering candlelight. Who lit a candle?

Robert could see the outline of her dark bush through her white panties. Virginia prowled onto the bed and up his legs. She reached Robert's waistline and unbuttoned his jeans. He helped her pull his pant legs over his feet. Then she was on his lap. Rocking, gyrating. His hands, up and down her rubbery body.

Then Robert opened his eyes. Virginia did the same. Robert saw inside those muddy, lightless eyes. Something in his brain popped. His body went rigid. His pelvis stopped thrusting. A cold grip wrapped around his cock. Nothing, there was nothing inside.

God was not in this room. Neither was Melissa.

Was it the acid? The marijuana? The bottle of Absolut? No. It was the F-man Himself. He had settled into the bed.

"What's wrong?" Virginia asked.

"Nothing," said Robert. He tried to kiss her again, but his lips were numb.

"I'm sorry," he said. "I can't..."

Virginia chased him to the door. Screamed at him from her front stoop. Robert had to walk home. The glorious sun, cresting over the horizon, gave the sky a pastel glow. His mom was up when Robert got home.

I crossed the lake. I climbed the waterfall. I rose up.

Robert pulled a pack of cigarettes out of the breast pocket of his flannel shirt. He popped a cig between his lips. He rolled down the window of the Honda and rain spattered in. He lit the cigarette.

She was just doing what she was trained to do. Poor Virginia. That was all she knew. Sex, sex, sex. That's what men and women do. You find a hole that's open and you hump it. Building a love is a waste of time. What happens after the months, years of building that relationship? The important things you gotta worry about. Stock options. Tax cuts. Mortgage payments. You gotta have the right clothes. The right car. The right computer. And once in a while, you gotta have a hole to hump.

Everything is going to be all right.

So, what can you do about it? Seems like everyone has the answer. The politicians have all the answers. The priests have all the answers. The brokers have all the answers.

But who gave them the answers? If everyone has the answers, who asks the question?

The doctors have the answers. The biologists, the chemists, the physicists, they all know the answers. The computer hacks know it too.

But who told them? Who gave them the code? If everyone is preaching so much, who do they listen to?

Everything's going to be all right.

Sure. Then let's go. Here we go.

Robert flicked his cigarette butt out the window. The door whirred as the glass eased up, cutting out the rain. The Honda Accord swerved a moment, and then Robert was back in control. He glanced down at the speedometer. Seventy-five miles-per-hour.

How much faster can I go? Robert asked himself. *You can always go faster. The faster I go, the quicker I will get there. I'll show them. Give them something to listen to. They'll never see me coming... but I should be heading back.*

A glow of headlights appeared ahead coming over the hill in the oncoming lane of Highway 20. Robert flicked off his brights. The oncoming car did not comply. Robert flashed his brights a couple of times in succession. He raised his hand to shield his eyes. So bright, he couldn't see the road.

Holy shit, what lane was he in? The car sped closer. Robert laid on his horn. Lights, smash. Boom, crash. Rat-a-tat.

Everything's going to be all right. Who's the rock star? What more can you ask for. Much more the plan.

Nothing but the Fucking-man Himself.

44

— • —

Epilogue

The Girl at the Bar

September 13, 1996

There she sat, a leopard frog on a lily pad. Sipping at her Bama slammer and glancing at her watch. Twelve-thirty. She had staked her table at Slim's two hours ago. Was he going to come? Her palms were damp. She had made three trips to the bathroom to reapply lip gloss and deodorant. Yet her armpits still glistened under her sleeveless blouse and slipped in deluginal crapulation.

The girl was a sophomore at Western U. She didn't usually go to bars. She grew up just west in a small farm town where weekends were spent cooking, cleaning, feeding cows, and attending church. She never drank alcohol until this summer when the other counselors at Bible camp dared her to try beer.

But this was the year she would climb out of her shell. So now she went to bars. The girl's friend, Maxie, was seated across from her at the table. Some guy leaned over next to Maxie. Maxie guffawed at his drunken repartee. His gap-toothed laugh made his chin disappear into the folds of his neck. His North Carolina hat was backwards, just like every other guy here.

The DJ was blasting "Back That Ass Up." This was the only song that the girl usually got up to dance for because she could certainly back her ass up. Otherwise, she preferred to sit in the corner and sip on her cocktail and look at him. The red-headed boy with the gapped teeth. Stare at him. Willing him to look back at her. Once in a while, he returned her gaze. Those blue heavenly eyes. His eyes never focused on whoever he was talking to and laughing with, they darted this way and that. Searching.

They did focus on hers. Deep and penetrating. You could see his soul in his eyes. That is what the French say. You can see a person's soul through their eyes. His eyes were blue and beautiful. Dripping with a pain and sorrow that she could soothe. She wanted to hold his head, stroke her hands through his thick red hair. Cradle his head to her heaving breast, still running her hands through his gorgeous mane.

Then life would be good.

Why was he not here? He was here every night. Usually with that big Mexican guy. The way he would just sit there, smirking, observing, judging, drinking, corrupting, conspiring, convincing her of the greatness that lurked within.

Tonight was the night she would talk to him. All the other girls did. Sometimes he would grab their ass. If only he would grab her ass. She could be his girl.

She had squeezed into her constricting leather mini skirt in hopes that he would... look at her ass. She bought the skirt at the mall. The last time she bought a skirt was to sing her solo with the church choir. This leopard-print skirt made her stomach ache, but it was worth it.

She looked down at her white thighs. She didn't like the way they fleshed out over the stool. She should be standing up. This was only her second slammer, but her head was revolving in a foggy whirl.

Maxie's bleach-blonde head weaved into her sight.

"Let's go dance," shouted Maxie.

"M'kay. I'm going to stay here."

"C'mon. You've been sitting here moping all night," whined Maxie. "Look, he's not coming. So come have some fun."

The exhilarated ape with the powder blue Tar Heels hat was grinning at Maxie's side.

"I'm all right," the girl said. "I'm fine here."

Her words slurred more than she would have liked.

"Whatever," said Maxie. She grabbed the Tar Heels boy's hand and led him through the gyrating mob.

The girl stood up. Her iced drink chilled her palm. Her steps were shaky. Her legs didn't work as well as she would have liked when they were bound together like plastic wrap. She made it to the bar. There was an empty stool on the end that she slumped into. Other customers stood around in clumps, trying to get the bartender's attention, squeezing forward, grimaces of frustration molded on their faces.

The girl's straw sputtered as she finished her drink. The ice had turned pink from the dosage of grenadine. She nudged the empty glass forward. She wanted to lay her head on her hands there on the bar, but this wasn't the time nor the place.

The bartender, Pete, came to her, ignoring the other curmudgeons. Even though he didn't know her name, Pete had always treated her well.

"Do you want another?" asked Pete, emptying her ice in the basin and tossing her straw in the trash.

"Sure," she said.

"Same thing?" he asked.

"Yeah," she said. "Alabama slammer."

She watched Pete make the drink through her drooping eyes. Her long, glazed eyelashes hung in front of her vision.

"Three bucks," said Pete, sliding the velvet red drink in front of her.

"Can I... ask a question?" said the girl. She pawed through her purse and pulled out the cash.

"Sure," said Pete with a shrug.

"Who's that red-haired guy that usually comes in here?"

"Who?"

"That red-haired guy. He's your friend. He comes here," said the girl, wishing to God her voice wasn't slurring like so. "I don't see him."

"You mean Robert?"

"Is that his name?"

"Yeah, he's a real fuckin' peach," said Pete, who picked up some pint glasses and started wiping them down vigorously.

"Is he... is he going to come tonight?" asked the girl.

"No," said Pete, eyes down. "Robert's dead."

Pete swiped the girl's money off the bar. He turned his back to her and addressed another customer.

A brick. A brick smashed the girl's heart. She stumbled from the bar stool, drink in tow. Her eyes welled up. She set her glass down on the nearest table. Blindly, she navigated her way through the orgasmic mob.

She found the back door. She pushed on the bar. Fresh air blasted her face as she stumbled into the back alley.

She sat down on the concrete. She felt her leopard miniskirt rip. She laid her face on her knees and bawled like Little Ann.

Nick Narigon

About the Author

On February 2, 1998, Nick Narigon and his friend Micheal Mosley drove from Cedar Falls, Iowa, to Boston Massachusetts. They had both dropped out of the University of Northern Iowa before completing their first semester. They lived in Boston for nine months. It was there that Nick started writing this book. After Boston, Nick spent four months in San Diego and three months working as a canoe guide in the Boundary Waters. He finally enrolled at the University of Iowa for the fall semester of 1999, graduating in 2003 with a B.A. in journalism. It was during this time that Nick completed the first draft of *The F-Man Himself*. He shared that draft with close friends and then let it sit on the shelf for 20 years. In the meantime Nick enjoyed a career as a journalist in America and Japan. In 2021 he and his family moved to Singapore in the middle of the coronavirus pandemic. In Singapore, Nick rediscovered the manuscript for *The F-Man Himself*. A stay-at-home-dad, he completed the manuscript and published it to share this story with those who wish to imbibe.

HAYSEED PRESS